The Nargun and the Stars
PATRICIA WRIGHTSON

The swamp, nestled among the mountains of Wongadilla, seemed the perfect place to hide. Here, high above the ranch of his middle-aged cousins, Simon was safe from their unwanted kindnesses, their mute offerings of friendship which reminded Simon that he was here against his wishes. Here because his parents were dead and there was nowhere else to go. But as Simon began to explore the swamp, he slowly realized that he was not alone. In the waters of the swamp and the dense foliage of the trees lurked strange creatures, spirits who haunted the land and played tricks on the men who thought the swamp and mountains were theirs by right. And there was something more—something ancient, without remorse or human pity. The Nargun, a creature as old as the earth and as lonely as the distance between the stars, had arrived in Wongadilla. And without realizing what he was doing, Simon had angered the Nargun and had given the Nargun his name. Now when night fell, the creature called to Simon without words, called his rage and loneliness —and the promise that he was coming.

"The author, probably mixing primordial tribal legends with the driving force of her own imagination, has written a strong and memorable book. The reader finds his senses sharpened by the precise images. The characters, seemingly plain and uncomplicated people, subtly come to life as complex human beings; and the essentially simple plot is worked into the rich fabric of a story that begins serenely, arches up to a great crescendo of suspense, and then falls away at the end to 'a whisper in the dark.'" —*Horn Book*

Also by Patricia Wrightson

A Little Fear

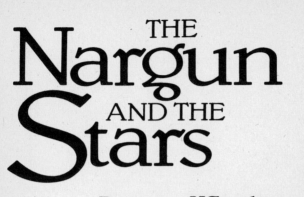

THE
Nargun
AND THE
Stars

Patricia Wrightson

PUFFIN BOOKS

PUFFIN BOOKS
Published by the Penguin Group
Viking Penguin Inc., 40 West 23rd Street, New York, New York 10010, U.S.A.
Penguin Books Ltd, 27 Wrights Lane, London W8 5TZ England
Penguin Books Australia Ltd, Ringwood, Victoria, Australia
Penguin Books Canada Ltd, 2801 John Street, Markham, Ontario, Canada L3R 1B4
Penguin Books (N.Z.) Ltd, 182–190 Wairau Road, Auckland 10, New Zealand

Penguin Books Ltd, Registered Offices: Harmondsworth, Middlesex, England

First published in the United States of America by Margaret K. McElderry Books/
Macmillan Publishing Company, 1974
Published in Puffin Books, 1988
Copyright © Patricia Wrightson, 1970
All rights reserved
Printed in the United States of America
by R. R. Donnelley & Sons Company, Harrisonburg, Virginia
Set in Times Roman

Library of Congress Cataloging in Publication Data
Wrightson, Patricia.   The Nargun and the stars.
Summary: An ancient stone creature threatens the lives of a family on a lonely sheep farm
in Australia.
[1. Fantasy.   2. Australia—Fiction]   I. Title.
[PZ7.W959Nar 1988]   [Fic]   87-35817
ISBN 0-14-030780-X

To Penny and James,
who live near Wongadilla;
and with thanks to Jill,
who sent me to the Nargun's den.

Map by Noela Young

Nargun Gully

Nyols Caves

Bulldozer

Bulldozed Forest

Woolshed

Wongadilla Boundary

Road to Town

THE
Nargun
AND THE
Stars

Prologue

IT WAS NIGHT *when the Nargun began to leave. Deep down below the plunging walls of a gorge, it stirred uneasily. It dragged its slow weight to the mouth of its den; its long, wandering journey had begun.*

Two hundred feet above, on the broad uplands, moonlight whitened the gum trees where eagles were building. It spilled into the gorge to touch the tallest heads of coachwood and nettle tree, but it never reached the black, damp rocks of the bottom. Only where water slid over the great slab of cliff at the head of the gorge, a glint of silver light was carried down.

At the bottom the water fell, with a sound-and-echo like guitar strings, into a pool that spanned the gorge. Behind this pool—behind a bead curtain of falling water—cut broad and low into the base of the cliff was the archway of a cave. This was the ancient den of the Nargun. Here it had lain while eagles learned to fly and gum trees to blossom; while stars exploded and planets wheeled and the earth settled; while the cave opened; while dripping water hollowed a pool from rock and filled it, and drop by drop built crystal columns before the cave. And all this while the Nargun slept.

In time it opened slow eyes and saw light. Little by little it dragged itself from earth and moved. There came a night when it had a voice and cried down the gorge. There came a day when, crouching in shadows, it grasped at something warm and found food to mumble on. After that it ate when it could: sometimes once in ten years, sometimes in fifty.

It moved down the gorge to blink at the sun, to watch a river flow, to hunt savagely; but always it made the ponderous climb back, crushing ferns and grinding moss on its way, to drag itself behind the crystal columns.

Sometimes it remembered the world's making and cried for that long agony. Sometimes it felt anger: for a fallen tree, a dried-up pool, an intruder, or for hunger. Then too it cried. It had a sort of love: a response to the deep, slow rhythms of the earth; and when it felt the earth's crust swell to the pull of the moon, it sometimes called in ecstasy. It had no fear; but a wide sunny place, or any strange thing, made it uneasy. Then it crouched in stony stillness, and little lizards ran over it.

Earth swung like a moth around the sun; time passed, and the shadows of the gorge thinned as the forests thinned above. By day the sun came slanting halfway down, and the Nargun crouched and hid. No food came *that way any more. Worse still, there was sometimes a strange tremor in the rocks, a vibration that was not the earth's. The old thing was restless and brooding. Earth, the soft-winged moth, flew round and round the sun and the Nargun's uneasiness grew; until this night.*

By now the crystal columns had grown into a fretted screen. The black bulk of the Nargun loomed beside it, peering through strands of water at a narrow path of stars. The sound of falling water was as clear as stars; it faltered as it always did when the old thing lurched through. Around the pool and down its ancient track the Nargun lumbered, rocking stiffly from one squat limb to the other. At the mouth of the gorge it crouched awhile and then, for the first time since earth was new, moved very slowly into the moonlit valley. It cried out once in anger or distress and headed north.

That was about 1880 and in Victoria in the south of Australia.

The Nargun blundered up the valley, blindly seeking: a gorge, deep and dark and filled with rain-forest, but where there was food and where the earth kept to its old rhythms. It found a gully and lumbered in, seeking and not finding. It met a rocky wall and slowly turned back. The moon set. In darkness the old dark thing moved on. Sometimes it went on all fours, sometimes crookedly erect, a relentless, heavy fumbling along the valley wall. It found another gully and crept in among ridges. Gray daylight came; it pressed itself into the side of the gully, still as stone.

When daylight turned to moonlight, it stirred and moved again, through a shallow creek, rumbling heavily among stones; partway up a low ridge. So it went on, night after night; up branching gullies yard by yard, and foot by foot up ridges. By day it crouched half-buried in the earth or among rocks. It bore the weight of the sun and the hardness of rain. By night it crept on blindly, and when it met a rock face or too steep a ridge it blundered blindly back.

Slowly, relentlessly, it worked its way north. By the end of the century it was near Bombala. Here it killed. They found a heap of torn and mangled clothing weeks after the old thing had passed.

Creeping up gullies and low ridges, by slow degrees the Nargun was led higher. It lumbered in the lower ranges, passing by the eastern end of the Australian Alps. They heard its cry in Cooma.

Year by slow year, rocking on stumpy limbs, it made its way north between the Shoalhaven and the range. There its claws left marks in rock that have never been explained. Always it traveled by night and lay like a stone by day. East of Lake George it killed again, a horse and a dog. By the 1920s it reached Goulburn and broke through eastward along the Wollondilly.

The next thirty years were a bad time for the Nargun, a time of blind uneasiness and sudden, sullen rage. Step by step, it stumbled along the fringes of the Blue Mountains, sensing the nearness of gorges and frustrated by vertical heights. The vibrations here drove it from un-

easiness to anger—the throbbing of some shaken, uneven pulse that was strange. The thing killed four times on this stretch: twice for food, leaving torn garments that rotted and were never found; twice in sudden, crushing rage, a man and a boy.

Aimlessly driven by its blind need, it blundered north between spurs of the Hunter Range. It crept through Singleton on a night when the electricity had failed, and no one in that town knew what went by rocking from limb to limb in the starlight. Northward still into tangled ranges, where its need drove it with painful slowness up long slopes that the trees rode like a swing.

Between the Mitchell and the Hunter, in seventy years of crawling, it had found no gorge chiseled through level uplands; and so the Nargun dragged itself by western slopes up ridges, and yard by yard and year by year up spurs. It saw the heights setting their rocky shorelines to the wind, and though it never reached them it inched its way up. It heard the howl of space in the wind and felt its tides and currents. It lifted its craggy head and howled back. Once it saw the moon lean down to touch a mountain. Once or twice it killed a beast.

In the 1960s it turned west along a range. It knew this range from ancient times, knew it had been poured molten from rose-red fires hoarded within the earth. From Ben Hall's Gap to Crawney Pass, slowly it untied the tangled knot of ridge and spur. Across blue distance it saw the slow world turning, and in high shadowed hollows felt the white sting of snow. Once it glimpsed, in a great far

7

cliff, the turquoise granite of a mountain's bones. Crouching in rain, it heard the shout of a waterfall.

One night, rocking its slow way around a mountain, it lumbered into a cleft cut downward through the mountain's crown. It was shaded and cool with a trickle of water, and it opened into a shallow gully blocked with brambles. There were ferns and moss, and a way through the brambles to hunt. The ancient Nargun rested there. It had come to Wongadilla.

Wongadilla received it with a stillness of water, a silence of trees, and a stirring within rocks. Its own ancient creatures sensed the Nargun that had come so far. They knew its age—ten times their own—and its slow, monstrous coldness. They stirred or were silent, like children.

Wongadilla is one knot in that tangle of spurs and ridges. You would say it is much like the other small sheep-runs nearby, but Charlie claims it is greener. Its steepest, sharpest height is called "the mountain," but really it is a clump of high and higher tops melted together in one. There are green places high and low, and slopes of tall grass the color of moonlight; shade trees everywhere, and a patch or two of scrub, and rock breaking through in the steepest places.

Halfway down its looming height, the mountain spreads a broad lap and from there throws out three ridges into the flat between it and the opposite mountain. One of these is near the eastern end of the mountain, like a long arm running out from under its rocky shoulder.

This ridge is covered in forest and lies half in Wongadilla and half outside it; Charlie's boundary fence, running down the mountain, cuts across the ridge and through the forest and takes in the flat below. The flat spreads wide between this ridge and the other two, like the space between your thumb and your first two fingers.

The other two ridges lie close together, holding between them a narrow, deep gully where the creek runs down to the river. Where they join the mountain is the round green swelling of a hill, and behind this a hollow that is always green with a glint. This is the swamp. When you come on it, hidden on the side of the mountain and halfway up to the crest of the wind, then you begin to know Wongadilla.

If you go into the swamp, you feel no squish of mud but rough clean water-couch springing under your toes. Rafts of pink-tipped weed drift with the wind, drawing its pattern in lines on the water. Jelly-froth rafts of frog-spawn are moored to tufts of bull grass, for the swamp is always loud with the creaking and hiccuping of frogs. There are rootled-out, snuffled-up holes where a wombat was feeding—a tuft of clean mauve fur left by a swamp-wallaby—it is like seeing a door close as someone slips away. And something else lives in the swamp: something sly and secret, half as old as the mountain. On a still day you may hear it chuckle.

Clinging to the mountainside above the swamp is another patch of forest. Its steep ground, bare except for dead leaves, is terraced by roots into shallow steps going up the mountain. In this forest, and in the one on the end ridge, you may be showered with twigs from swinging treetops. For every rabbit, lizard, or bandicoot that rustles through the dead leaves, you may hear two—just as in the swamp you may see the swirl of an eel or hear a chuckle. There are ancient tricksters in the trees of Wongadilla as well as in the swamp. They were silent and uneasy when the Nargun came, only rustling restlessly as they listened for its voice. After a year or so of waiting and hearing no call, they came scuttling and gliding from the forest tops to nearer trees. They pelted it with sticks and hissed when the sticks came flying back. After that, they kept away from the slow, cold monster in the gully.

On the second of the mountain's three ridges stands a white house with a red brick chimney—below the swamp, far under the wall of the mountain, but high and straight above creek and flat. Charlie Waters and his sister Edie live in the white house. They are old now, but they were children there. From the house a track leads down, back and forth across the steep, blunt end of the ridge and over a bed of stones in the river just below the point where the creek joins it. The river itself is hardly more than a creek, even after rain; but not even Charlie or Edie would try the crossing after one hour's rain, in case the river rolled their old station wagon over. It is a small river, but quick with the weight of the mountain behind it.

The track joins a gravel road that finds its way in from the valley, running over the toes of opposing hills. Along this road, splashing through the river, and swinging with-

out a thought up the narrow, dangerous track, Charlie drove the station wagon on the day he and Edie brought Simon Brent, the sullen boy who was a stranger, to Wongadilla. The dogs heard them coming and barked and leaped about at the ends of their chains.

1

NO ONE COULD have been stranger than Simon. He was a
stranger even to himself, and he had never heard of
Wongadilla till a few days before. He was at the Home
then, and he still felt raw all over, as if he had been
skinned—all the known things, all his known life,
suddenly torn away. Gone in twenty seconds, or however
long it takes for one car to crash into another. One great
WHOOMP!—and Simon Brent, who never heard it, who
was in fact playing football at the time, had become a
stranger with no world of his own.

He didn't even know; he had just gone on playing football; would you believe that? At the Home he sometimes
woke up shivering: he had probably been getting that
pass off to Flinty, or tackling the ratbag with the ginger
hair, when the car crashed with Mum and Dad. And *he
had gone on doing it,* till they came out on the field and
told him to stop.

He had been at the Home for weeks and weeks before he heard of Wongadilla. That was only the other day, when he came in from the new strange school.

". . . Miss Edith Waters, Simon, your mother's second cousin . . ."

And there was Edie, stout on top with skinny legs, wearing a bunchy green coat with a brown fur-thing over it and a pair of brown felt wings perched on her gray-and-black hair. She looked something like a green leghorn and nothing at all like his smooth young mother.

". . . a sheep-run in the mountains. She and her brother want you to go and stay with them and make it your home if you're happy there. . ."

"Do I call you Auntie Edith?" he asked gruffly, because they were waiting for him to speak. She didn't answer at once, so he looked at her. She had a creamy face, like wilting petals, and sudden gray eyes. He looked away quickly from that sudden glimpse of a person watching him from the gray eyes.

She said, "Edie'll do me and Charlie'll do Charlie, but I suppose you might want to put an auntie and uncle between us. Suit yourself."

So he didn't call either of them anything.

He asked about the place. "Wongadilla," she told him. "Five thousand acres, right up the Hunter." She didn't tell him any more about it or what fun they would have or how well she remembered his mother. She was still, like a swamp. He hardly knew why he agreed to go—except that one Home was as good as another, and he couldn't

13

stay at this one if they wanted him to go. Mrs. Brown of the Home was the enthusiastic one.

"It sounds wonderful, Simon! A boy in the country—a family of your own—you'd like to try it, wouldn't you?"

He said yes, still gruffly. He was mostly gruff these days.

They came by train, Simon wedged in a corner by the window, watching the world grow wide and empty, the color of hay under a widening sky, endless wire fences and blue hills lifting. Sometimes for relief he changed the focus of his eyes and looked instead at reflections in the window: his own thin face with heavy brown hair and sullen brown eyes—and the green-and-brown ghost of Edie hanging in the glass behind him.

They got out at a station in a little flat town, and Charlie was there to meet them. He was taller and thinner than anyone Simon had ever seen. He had gray-and-black hair and sudden gray eyes like Edie's and in other ways was the exact picture of what an Australian country man is supposed to be. His face was brown and lined; he wore his mouse-colored old felt hat like a lid, and a faded blue shirt, a hand-knitted sweater, and drill trousers washed to a creamy shade.

Charlie said, "*There* you are."

Edie said, "*Here* we are."

They exchanged a light, ceremonial kiss and Charlie clapped Simon on the shoulder. Then he picked up two suitcases in each hand and led the way out to his old cream station wagon.

It was a long drive from the station on a road that

sometimes broke into astonishing colors: patches of turquoise or fuchsia gravel, banks that glowed coral-red in the sun. Flocks of gray cockatoos swept up from the road, turning to clouds of pink as they rose. Charlie told Edie scraps of news about sheep, dogs, a horse, and a neighbor. Tall hills and ridges advanced and retreated, turned about and changed places, in a great, slow Morris dance. High rocks and shadowy hollows hung with blue; green humps and ridges; slopes the color of hay or of moonlight; the frown of forests.

"They'll be clearing scrub on the end ridge," said Charlie. "Taking out the bit of timber that's worth it. Brought a bulldozer up yesterday."

Edie made a disgruntled sound. "We'll be having some noise, then," she said.

And what's wrong with a bit of noise? thought Simon sullenly. He had never been so far into the country before, and the close, insistent noise of just one engine was making his ears feel funny. Sometimes they passed a house, and Charlie and Edie always looked at it with attention. Simon thought that a single house amid crowding hills was about the loneliest thing in the world.

After more than an hour of driving, they splashed through a stream, stopped at a gate, and went on up a ridge. Above the sound of the climbing motor came the clamor of dogs. They had reached Wongadilla, a single house among crowding hills. Charlie put his head out of the window. "All right, *put a sock in it.* LIE DOWN!" he roared. The dogs dropped their voices to an eager whimper, the engine stopped—and there was the silence waiting, coiled like a spring between earth and sky.

There were sounds, often startling, but they never did set off the coiled-spring trap of the silence. The dogs still whimpered, hens clucked behind the house, a magpie's call rang like a bell. Somehow the silence took these sounds and out of them built more silence. A hard, nasal cry, distant but sharp, made Simon jump.

"Old ewe," said Charlie, handing him a suitcase. "Edie'll have the kettle boiling. I could do with a cup, what about you?"

They had tea in the kitchen where a big stove burned day and night. Edie had already put away her green coat, brown fur, and winged hat; she now wore a red-and-black frock and a green hand-knitted sweater. The house was old and full of old things. There was a row of bedrooms opening onto a long veranda where Charlie and Edie had their rooms, but Simon's was a tiny one just off the living room. White walls stood close to the bed; there was a red felt mat on the polished wood floor, and a great dark old pine outside the cobwebbed window.

He put his things away where Edie showed him and went out slowly feeling lost and sore, as if he had been carried off out of the world; hating it and the strangers who acted as if it were normal. They must be mad already, he thought, or they'd go mad here.

Charlie was in the living room, lighting a fire in the brick fireplace. Its yellow light flickered across Simon's bedroom door. A jarring of crazy laughter came from outside. "Kookaburra," said Charlie, settling a log in place.

"I know *that*," said Simon. They were his first words at Wongadilla.

No one told him where to go or what to do, so he wandered out to the kitchen where Edie was cooking. She flicked a look at him. "You'll want an early night," she said.

I don't want anything in this weird place, thought Simon savagely.

He had to do something, so he followed Charlie outside and stood about while Charlie fed fowls, dogs, and horses and milked cows. The western hills were so high and near that the sun had gone behind them already. The air was sharp and cool. From far down on the flat came a wild cry, half animal and half human. Simon shivered.

"Fox," said Charlie instantly, from behind a cow. "Too many of *them* about."

He wandered inside again. Edie was peeling potatoes and spoke into the kitchen sink. "You could have a bath before dinner if you liked and be ready for bed. Your things are warming by the fire. That's old Pet neighing."

He needed to know but was not glad to be told, and it made him angry to find his pajamas, robe, and slippers beside the fire like a baby's. Even the bathroom looked make-believe, with the old bath standing on its four feet on bare boards. He had washed and was getting into his pajamas when—CRASH! The breath rushed out of him, the house shook and echoed, and Simon was standing rigid in the kitchen doorway clutching his robe.

Charlie was closing the lid of a large wooden chest in a corner of the kitchen. He and Edie stared at Simon.

"Filling the woodbox," they said together, guiltily. Simon marched back to the bathroom. That was it, then; nothing was going to shock him like that again. From now on he would expect anything and question nothing.

They had chops, mashed potatoes, and pumpkin at a table in the kitchen. Edie said, "This is your place . . . Simey," and it took him a moment to realize that she was talking to him. "Eat what you can and leave the rest," she added. "That's a wallaby thumping."

"Or an old 'roo," said Charlie, heaving his chair into place.

After dinner they sat round the living room fire and listened to the news. Edie sat on one side, moving her rocking chair just a little with a soft, regular creak. She had brought out some bright blue wool to knit a sweater for Simon. Charlie sat in an old leather chair on the other side of the fire, his feet in socks stretched out on the hearth almost into the ashes. Simon was in the middle, in an old cane chair that kept up a conversation of whispered squeaks. A train-rhythm was beating in his head, and the red coals made hill-shapes endlessly changing. He leaped awake when something heavy thudded on the roof with a hideous scratching of claws on iron.

"Possums," said Charlie and Edie at once. Edie added, "There's a hot-water bag in your bed when you're ready."

Simon went to bed, closing his door. He was almost too tired to sleep. Every time he closed his eyes the hill-shapes advanced, retreated, turned and swung, till he opened them again and looked at darkness. The pine tree outside his window breathed quietly in the wind, and outside something called with a menacing *oom—oom—oom*. Then the catch of his door clicked, and it opened a little. Warm yellow firelight flickered in the opening; Simon watched it till he fell asleep.

A half-moon slipped down behind a spur. Below the shoulder of the mountain a blunt yellow machine stood under the stars. Sly eyes peered at it from out of the tops of trees.

It was late when Simon woke, and Charlie was already away working on the mountain. From time to time the sound of his work came down to the house, *thunk! thunk! thunk!* Simon would have liked to ask what he was building up there, but he could not yet say "Charlie."

He was eating a special late breakfast when a sound he did know came from the mountain: the hoarse, rumbling shout of a heavy machine. Edie lifted her head. "They've started, then," she said; and Simon remembered what Charlie had said about a bulldozer clearing scrub. His heart lifted a little. There were men with a big machine just up there.

Since no one told him where to go or what to do he spent the morning wandering around the house, gazing at the deep, dark gully with its creek far down on one side, the flat far down on the other, and the forested ridge that climbed up from it to the mountain's shoulder. He spent a lot of time looking up there, though he could not see the bulldozer because of the forest in between. He would have liked to climb up there but thought he would probably need permission; it was really quite a long way and only looked close because the mountain was so high. He couldn't bring himself to ask Edie and dreaded being scolded for going without asking. So he had to be satisfied with listening to the bulldozer: its shout rising to a roar when it attacked something and dropping to a grumble when it backed away. Sometimes there was an enormous slow breaking sound and then a long crash, and he knew that a tree had fallen. Sometimes the bulldozer stopped, and the silence came springing back with its spare, precise erection of sounds: the *thunk! thunk! thunk!* of Charlie's work; birdcalls; wind among leaves. Then would come a flat, solid *boom!* that Simon guessed was blasting; another tree would begin its long, slow crash, and then the bull-dozer would start again.

After lunch Simon did slip away without asking. Edie was watering roses, her ankles jutting sharply above cracked old gardening shoes. He told himself angrily that she couldn't keep him hanging about the place forever, that there had to be somewhere he could *go*. He could see a patch of trees on the mountain above the gully and a glimpse of road below it. He slipped quietly away to walk across there.

And so, in a hollow just below that scrub, Simon discovered the swamp.

He could hardly believe it, lying there so secret and so high. He thought there must have been rain lately, and soon the water would drain away. Yet it must have been there a long time for the flat-floating leaves of water-parsley to spread so far. And at one end, nearest the gully, there was a broken bank of earth where someone had once tried to turn the swamp into a dam; dried stems of purple-top stood five feet tall on the bank, and the deeper water there was fringed with reeds browned by winter. The tuneless, changeless song of frogs might have been going on since the world was made.

There was a chuckling noise; something splashing in the water, probably. Simon took off his shoes and walked into the swamp.

The Potkoorok stirred. Its golden eyes gleamed. It slid like a ripple through the water, watching the boy. It waited while he explored the edges, examining brilliant green moss with air bubbles trapped in it. It waited while he scooped up tiny slate-blue tadpoles and examined them and let them go. It waited till he stepped into deeper water; then it curled a coldness around his ankle, slithering like an eel.

Simon gave a yell and leaped onto a tussock. There was a stick caught there; he grabbed it and poked and prodded, peering into the water. There was no sign of anything. It must have been a strand of moss that wound itself around his ankle. He began to feel stupid about having yelled and stepped off his tuft. There was a watery gurgle as if the swamp chuckled. Simon went striding through the bull grass, sending water-spiders darting away.

The swamp-creature smiled slyly. It knotted two tufts of grass together and waited. A boy was the accident of a moment, something as light and brief as a sun-glint on water—but a good trick was something to chuckle over for a hundred years. It waited easily.

Simon got over his fright and forgot to feel foolish. The swamp was rich and exciting, a place of his own tucked away privately between mountain and hillock. He had found some small black worms lashing about in wet earth. He pored over them, wondering what kept them in this state of struggle. After that he looked at some frog-spawn; the black specks of embryos looked almost big enough to hatch. He went from one lot to the next looking for hatching tadpoles—until he took one more step and went sprawling forward.

He saved himself by splashing his hands down into bubbled weed and came up with weed clinging to his wet arms. He cleaned it off and looked to see what had tripped him. He saw the knotted tufts of grass. *That* couldn't be an accident, and it wasn't something an animal could do. He splashed angrily back to firm ground, hearing again that low, watery chuckle.

"All right, you wait!" shouted Simon. He picked up a lump of wood and sent it skittering across the swamp.

The Potkoorok narrowed its golden eyes. So the boy

wanted to change the rules? He might have been puzzled or frightened or too stupid for either—instead, he had challenged the ancient joker. The Potkoorok accepted the challenge and caught the lump of wood before it sank. First the wood began to spin as if a whirlpool had caught it, then it whirled in circles around and around on the water. Faster and faster it went, until it dived under the water and disappeared. The swamp-creature had declared itself.

Simon stood and watched, frowning but refusing to give way, until the stick disappeared. Weird . . . weird . . . like this whole weird place. He put his shoes on to go back to the house, but after ten steps he turned around again. The swamp lay flat and innocent, with a secret glint of water between the bull grass. The hole at the end was dark and still among tall rushes.

"That's where it lives," he said to himself.

Whatever it was in the swamp, it was something different. Tricky . . . wild . . . not solid and dull like a grown-up stranger. More like another boy . . . He was a bit frightened, but he almost wanted to go back.

He didn't go back. The western hills were throwing shadows over the swamp; the shouting of the bulldozer had stopped some time ago, and now the *thunk! thunk! thunk!* of Charlie's work had stopped too. He walked back to the house while the hills' long shadows reached further and further to grasp him. He reached the rough track down the ridge and heard soft creakings and blowings and a thud of hoofs. Charlie was coming down from the mountain behind him on a big bay horse.

Simon stepped quickly off the track, but Charlie slowed the horse till it paced beside him. "Surprise won't stand on you," he said. "You just want to keep back of his head and go steady. So you found the swamp."

So much for being tucked away in a place of his own. Simon said, "It's always there, isn't it?"

"Gets a bit smaller in a dry spell, but it's always there."

"What lives in it, anyhow?"

"All sorts," said Charlie. "Frogs, of course. A few leeches. Pond snails—"

"What big thing?"

Charlie looked thoughtful. "Eel, maybe?" Simon said nothing to this; eels don't make grass-traps. Charlie said, "Hear them working on the scrub?"

"They don't work long," said Simon rather scornfully. "They start late and finish early."

"They've got to come out from town and go back at night," Charlie explained. "Takes a bit out of their day."

"What were you doing up there, anyhow?" said Simon, able to ask at last.

"Fencing," said Charlie. "I could do with a hand tomorrow, that's if you've got nothing better to do."

Simon considered. By then he would probably want to go back to the swamp—but he mightn't get another chance to see the bulldozer working. "All right," he said gruffly.

Charlie dismounted at the shed behind the house and

hitched Surprise to a post. "Might want him again if the cows don't come up. I could do with a cup, what about you?"

Simon followed him into the kitchen, refusing to look at Edie, waiting for her to say somethng about going off without asking. But she only said, "So you found the swamp. You could do with a cup, then. I've lit the fire."

"You're a bottler," said Charlie gratefully. "Isn't she, Simey?" Simon couldn't answer. If he opened his mouth, he knew, he would yell, *Don't call me that!* And what was the use? It would just make another name that nobody could say. They had to call him Simey; they were Edie and Charlie.

That night again the fire was too much for Simon. He was sleepy with sun and sharp air and distances. Edie sat in her rocking chair, creaking it a little back and forth and knitting his thick blue sweater. Charlie stretched his feet into the ashes and read the papers that the mail-car left every second day in the box beside the road. The cane chair carried on its tiny squeaking chatter; the flames danced like sunlight on swamp-water. From outside came that low, menacing *oom—oom—oom* that he had heard last night.

"Frogmouth," said Charlie absently, from behind the paper.

Sometimes Simon thought he could hear another sound: a sad, high howling, far away and lost. Once Edie lifted her head and frowned as if she heard it too. Yet

Simon could not be sure; it came and went like the wind, faint and far.

He listened for it while he climbed into bed and felt for the hot-water bag. Just as he fell asleep, he thought he heard it plainly.

2

NEXT DAY SIMON gave Charlie a hand with the fence, riding with him up the mountain on old Pet. No one mentioned Pet until he discovered her saddled at the shed beside Surprise—and stopped in his tracks, questions and alarms rolling about in his mind like marbles.

"Quiet old thing," said Charlie. "Like a table. You won't get any fancy riding, but she'll take you up there if you give her time. You'll want a leg up."

There was a moment of rushing upward, and Simon found himself perched in the saddle gripping the pommel with both hands.

"You want to hold on to her mane, not the saddle," Charlie advised, handing him the reins and shortening the stirrups. "Now all you've got to do is sit there, and not fall over the old girl's tail on the mountain."

This proved to be true. When Simon was used to Pet's lurching walk, he simply sat on her back while she followed Surprise up the ridge. Once or twice he guided her jerkily around a stone or stump, just to prove that he understood about reins and could do it. When they reached the steep rise, Charlie said, *"Now* you'll need those stirrups." Simon had thought he was using them already; but he stood up in them as Charlie did and leaned forward.

From around the end of the mountain came a sudden roar: the bulldozer had started. It was very near, but still out of sight around the curve of the mountain. Simon had no time for it yet. He was too busy with the mountain itself.

The trail wriggled up it like a snake, turning back and forth between a fence and a small gully. At every turn the horses heaved themselves heavily up to the next level. Soon the sound of the bulldozer was below. The world fell dizzily away into vistas of far blue ridges; the wind curled around the mountain with a dangerous pull. The end ridge was so far under that you looked down on the tops of the forest; they were rippling in the wind and roaring huskily like the sea. The complicated pattern of ridge and gully was flattened into a map, easy to see. The house was a white shoebox, with a small toy Edie walking across the yard. You could see a glint of the swamp, and its scrub, and a loop of road curling in toward them and out again. Simon felt as if he were perched on the brink of the world and might fall off if Pet stumbled. He could see past the end of the mountain and across the forest, new ridges tying Wongadilla into the tangle of ranges.

They stopped on a grassy ledge, with the mountain's top still looming above them. Charlie unsaddled the horses and tethered them in the shade among brambles and bracken, tall trees, and silver-gray logs. Charlie pulled out from under one log a sack containing tools and a coil of wire. Simon saw that some of the posts of the fence were rotted off at the bottom, so that they hung heavily on the wires they should have supported; and new iron posts were laid beside them. The posts were not very evenly spaced, probably because they had been put in wherever it was possible to sink a hole. It was hard to imagine how the fence had been built at all in such a place. From the fence, at last, you could look down the end of the mountain onto the bulldozer. Simon was startled at what it had done.

Already the bulldozer had wrecked a whole slice of forest. Slaughtered trees lay where they had fallen, or where they had been snigged aside. A few had been trimmed into logs and neatly stacked, and two men with a chain-saw were now trimming another. The yellow bulldozer worried at the edge of the forest like some great blunt beast, roaring above the howl of the chain-saw. Its snub yellow shape stood out clearly under the canopy that protected the driver. Simon watched it at work, while the wind tugged at him.

Near at hand came the *thunk! thunk!* that had come from a distance yesterday. Charlie had started work, he was setting a post in its hole by banging it with a mallet. Simon remembered that he was supposed to help.

As it turned out, there was nothing he could do except pass a tool and sometimes hold the end of a wire, but Charlie seemed to find this very helpful. "Say the word when you've had enough," he said, "and I'll put the saddle back on Pet for you. She'll take you home and glad of the chance."

"It's all right," grunted Simon. He knew "thank you" would have been better, so he added, "Which is your land?"

"This is one boundary," said Charlie, patting a post. "It takes you down to the road. But up by the swamp the road's got Wongadilla on both sides of it. To the top of the range and a bit down the other side, about five thousand acres. Not enough, and most of it standing on end." He looked down the mountain with exasperated pride and then sideways at Simon. His lined brown cheeks became blotched with pink. He made a sort of noise and said quickly, "It'll be yours some day if you want it."

Simon was terrified. To own this plunging country with its blue heights and cream-colored flanks and green depths—and the swamp! He headed off up the slope to recover.

He found he had started to climb the forehead of the mountain, and it was such hard work that he kept on. Sometimes he went up sideways by narrow ledges, sometimes climbing rocks and using hands as well as feet. Sometimes he could reach up to a hold on a bush or tree and pull himself higher. Once the shouting of the bulldozer stopped, and he planted himself against a rock to look down. The mountain sheltered him from the wind, though he could still hear it.

The bulldozer was hidden by the ledge where Charlie was working, but he saw two men come from the forest and run back out of sight. Silence—then that hard, flat *boom!*—and very slowly a tall treetop began to sway over. It made a great sweep across the forest that crowded behind it: slowly, down and down. There seemed to be no force in it, no reason for the cracking of branches and crying of leaves. The crash at the end seemed to go on for seconds while branches bounced and sprang. It was something to see and remember, the felling of a big tree. Simon hardly noticed himself climbing again till he found himself standing upright on humpy ground fringed with trees.

The wind leaped at him again and took away the little breath he had. This was the top, the very highest place on the mountain; he was standing on the top of Wongadilla. He would have liked to shout to it: "I'm up here! I'm on top of you!" But something in the silence of the ridges and spurs all around—a great quiet, like a roomful of giants thinking—kept him quiet too.

He walked across the hump, clambered down and around it a bit, and found that it dropped into a gully. He remembered the track snaking up the mountain between fence and gully: that was this gully, lower down where it was shallower. Climbing down into it he thought that he was getting to know the place a bit and was pleased with himself. He went down the gully to what he guessed was about Charlie's level. It was sheltered and quiet; he sat down to rest beside a great boulder that wore a blue-green lichen like a round lace mat.

Charlie must know every bit of Wongadilla, all the part that Simon had never seen. Even Edie. She had lived here all her life, though she never seemed to leave the house now. They must know where the creek started. Ages ago they must have played in the swamp. He picked up a stick and scratched his name in the lichen on the big rock: SIMON. There was no room for any more, so he scratched BRENT in another lichen on a small stone near the rock.

Suddenly he felt that this was something he should not have done—to scratch his name on the rocks of Wonga-dilla. Now the gully called to him silently: SIMON BRENT! He got up quickly and climbed out into the wind. The bulldozer had stopped, and it was Charlie who was calling.

"Simey!"

He was supposed to be helping Charlie! He climbed around the mountain as fast as he could—but it was only time for a cup of tea. Charlie had taken a large flask from a bag strapped to his saddle and was pouring tea into mugs. Down on the ridge the bulldozer men were also sitting in the shade with mugs.

"Had a good scramble?" said Charlie. "Better have one of Edie's coconut biscuits, she'll be hurt if we take them home."

After that Simon stayed on duty, wordlessly holding wire and passing tools, keeping an eye on the bulldozer.

When they stopped for the lunch that Edie had packed, the other men stopped too, as if there were some rule about everyone stopping at once. Even when the fence was finished early, and Charlie was leading the way down the mountain with the sack of tools in front of him on the saddle, the bulldozer stopped too. Simon heard again the waiting silence.

It was much worse riding down the mountain than up. At every turn of the track it was like stepping down from the sky. Charlie said it was hard on the horses too. It was good to reach easier slopes where you could see the ground in front and where, as the track came close to the fence, Simon saw the bulldozer parked for the night. Its driver, a blunt young man in a navy singlet and shorts, called out to them.

"Knock-off time?" shouted the bulldozer man. Leaning on the top wire of the fence he added, "Bit windy, isn't it?"

"Getting up," roared Charlie in reply. "Be a bit rough tonight."

"A bit rough last night too!"

Charlie looked surprised and reined in. Pet stopped obediently behind. "Eh?" said Charlie. "A bit of a breeze, that's all." There was a pause during which Charlie and the bulldozer man eyed each other in grave surprise like well-bred dogs. Simon took this chance to have a look at the bulldozer.

Those two things like brakes were really the steering, of course; one of them for each track. And those were the hydraulics, like gears, on the right. The chimney sticking up in front was really the exhaust, with the breadth of the muffler interrupting it. What would she sound like if the exhaust broke off under the muffler? Maybe it would, with luck; it looked a bit rusty. He remembered the shouting of the engine while it was still muffled, with the thin demon shrieking of the metal tracks (for lack of oil) rising above it; and he tried to imagine the monstrous din of the same engine without its muffler.

"Thought it was blowing hard," the bulldozer man was saying to Charlie. "The old 'dozer was covered in rubbish this morning—took me ten minutes to clean her out."

"That right?" said Charlie politely.

"Twigs, dead wood, branches—all small stuff. I thought, 'There's been a bit of wind.' "

"We never *noticed* any," said Charlie. "Nothing else disturbed?"

"Just the 'dozer. Funny, that."

They exchanged nods, and Charlie and Simon rode on. "Possums," Charlie confided to Simon. "He's left it under a tree full of possums."

When they reached the house, Edie was taking washing in. She had chained the clothes hoist to a post like a dog to keep it from whirling around and swinging her off her feet. Even so, it tugged at the chain and jerked her to and fro. She looked like a ruffled hen with its feathers blown the wrong way. A pillow slip flapped off into a bush and Simon had to chase it and bring it back.

"Thanks, Simey," she said, breathing hard. "That's the

last. The kettle's boiling, and we could all do with a cup."

She was surprised that the fence was finished, and Charlie said that an extra man made the difference, and it was a change having company. Simon turned pink, knowing he had not deserved this praise; so after the tea he went out again and passed things wordlessly while all the animals were fed.

As darkness came, the wind grew stronger. It came leaping from the western ridge and across the gully to shove at the house and spill past. It pushed at windows, cried in telephone wires, and blew sirens around the roof. It got into the ceiling and under the floor and drew the fire up the chimney like a corkscrew. It made the mat in Simon's room rise stealthily and creep about the floor. And whenever it paused for breath there was another sound: the sad, high howling of last night, much clearer now; high over the house and all around, everywhere and nowhere. It made Edie restless. She put down her knitting and shuffled her knobbly feet until Charlie lowered yesterday's paper and looked at her over its edge.

All that night the wind blew. Simon lay in the dark and listened: to the sirens in the roof and the stealthy slither of the mat along his floor, and the crying of the pine outside the window. Now and then in the night he woke and heard them still.

Toward morning the flood of wind ebbed away. The mat lay crumpled and still. The crying of the pine softened to a tall whisper against the stars. But that other sound, the howling like wild animals calling far away, swept over and round the house till dawn. The moon had set, but spindly shadows went flickering against the stars. One of them sprang from the top of the pine and was lost in the bulk of an ironbark thirty feet away.

From tree to tree the shadows went, leaping like sugar-gliders. They sprang from the highest branches, spreading their sticklike arms wide. Their long straggling beards streamed as they floated down to the trunks of farther trees, and the howling went with them. The spindly shadows swept over and around the house while Simon slept: the ancient Turongs of the fallen forest, looking for new homes.

Perhaps Simon heard them in his sleep, for he woke late again when Charlie was already away "around the sheep." At breakfast he remarked rather awkwardly that he thought he would go to the swamp.

Edie observed that he would like to take his lunch and have a decent day, and produced a lunch already cut from the refrigerator. She added that he would find old Pet saddled by the shed.

Simon turned pink.

"What if I—can't manage her?"

"Then you'll be no worse off," said Edie calmly. "You can knot the reins so they won't dangle and turn her loose. She'll come home."

"But *what if I fall off?*"

"You'll have your work cut out—unless you stand on your head in the saddle. Suit yourself—no need to take her if you'd rather not. But she'll stand for you all day if you throw the reins over a stump."

Simon rode old Pet with his lunch in a bag buckled to the saddle. Edie showed him a useful stump to mount by and handed him a stick from a sapling near the gate.

"You won't have Surprise to keep her going today," she said. "She won't move at all if you don't have a stick."

She started Pet off with a slap on the rump, and Simon aimed her in a general way up the ridge. It was stupid, he grumbled to himself, having to take Pet when it was such a short way. Why couldn't they just let him walk? He *liked* walking.

The wind was up again, but only in gusts. The bull-dozer was shouting on the mountain, sometimes mixed with the screaming of the chain-saw and the long-drawn *crack, swish, thud* of falling timber. The sounds were blown away and came sweeping back like sheets on a clothesline. Pet went very slowly, sometimes stopping altogether till Simon switched at her rump with the stick. After a while it felt high and free to be riding alone to the swamp. The outlines of windswept hills were hard and clear, and the sky behind them had a crystal shine. Shadows were sharp, and every leaf and twig exact. At the swamp the water was like rippled glass in the clear places. You could see the shape of the wind on it, in the windblown lines of moss and weed.

Simon scrambled down onto a log, dropped Pet's reins over a dead branch of it, and took off his shoes. He went straight to the bank at the far end, where dead purple-top rattled like castanets when the wind blew. He broke off a thick stalk of it and went down the bank to prod in the water.

The deep hole was still out of reach. He stepped into the water at the edge, swishing in front with his stick until he could lean forward and reach into the hole. The stick was instantly twitched out of his hand and disappeared. He waited, watching for it to float to the surface. It didn't.

He went back to the bank for another stalk and tried all over again, watching closely for just one glimpse of whatever it was that had taken his stick. Nothing happened. He prodded and swished for some time, first in the water and then at dead flower-heads on the reeds fringing the hole. He teased a water-boatman with the tip of his stick till it paddled off in a frantic zigzag. He trailed his stick toward another—and it was twitched out of his hand again and disappeared. The twitch was so forceful and sudden that it made him jump, but he saw nothing.

He tried skittering a stick over the place as he had last time, but nothing happened. The creature in the swamp was not to be tricked; it preferred to trick Simon. "*I* don't care, anyhow!" he shouted, and went stamping back to the shallow end to look for specimens and perhaps to think.

The swamp-creature felt more alive and tricky than it had for a long time. Its yellow-green skin gleamed as it slid through the swamp, and its throat bulged with silent chuckles. A boy who thought he could trick a Potkoorok!

When Simon was hungry, he took his lunch up into the

scrub. It was full of green-shadowed light and the sound of trees conversing with the wind. He sat on a wide terrace between roots and was at once showered with falling twigs and leaves. "Hey!" he said crossly, and brushed them off. Bulldozer noises were blown away and came billowing back. Whenever they were blown away, a different sound was blown to him from the opposite direction, a distant grumbling and clanking that seemed familiar. He puzzled about that between eating Edie's sandwiches and puzzling about the swamp-creature.

From time to time another shower of leaves and twigs rained down. He thought it was from the wind. They only stung a little, so he didn't bother to move. From time to time, too, there were rustlings of small paws scampering among leaves, but he could never see what made them.

The last thing in his lunchbox was an apple. He had taken one bite of it when two ideas clicked into his mind. One was that the odd sound coming and going on the wind was a grader; there must be one working along the road somewhere. The moment he recognized it he was able to stop thinking about that, and the second idea took over: a creature that could not be tricked might be coaxed. He gathered up his things at once and took his apple back to the far end of the swamp.

He laid the apple delicately on a tuft of broken reeds just under water at the edge of the deep hole. Standing a little way back, he kept his eyes on the apple.

Nothing happened. The wind blew and the weeds swung along its path. Now it blew the bulldozer noises to him and now the clanking of the grader. It made a green surf of the forest on the mountain. Glancing at the forest and from there along the mountain, Simon wondered if he could go by himself on old Pet to watch the bulldozer again. . . . Not up the steep part, of course, but just below it; the bulldozer must be nearly through to there by now. . . . Guiltily he looked down to the apple.

It was gone. He had been tricked again. While he stared with his mouth open, something was thrown that hit his shirt, splashed back into the water, and floated there. The apple core.

"You want to watch it!" Simon shouted angrily—and then he saw it. Just for a second something large and yellow-green shone as it turned through the water, and a golden eye winked. Clearly he heard the swamp's deep chuckle.

The Potkoorok loved an apple.

Simon pounced on the core. There were little tooth marks on it. He was suddenly charmed and full of wonder. He sat on the bank for a long time, but he didn't see it again.

Instead, with a great deal of grumbling and clanking and fussing, around a corner and along the road came the grader.

3

THE GRADER was a homely thing to see on the lonely loop
of road below the scrub. Like every grader Simon had
ever seen, it was orange-yellow, long and lanky, slow,
noisy, and fussy. It fumbled along, blade clanking and
grating on the gravel, and Simon ran around the swamp
to the nearest point to watch.

The grader also came to the nearest point. The driver,
who had a long, narrow face with a bristly chin, lifted two
fingers in the greeting of country drivers. Then, instead
of following the road around the loop, he began to turn
the machine. It backed clumsily, crept around, backed
again, with a lot more grumbling and clanking, to go
back over the section of road it had just done. Simon was
not surprised; he knew the habits of graders.

He was delighted to see that this one carried a warning
sign on the end of its blade: GRADER. He grinned, wondering how you were supposed to think it could be any-

thing else. It was a joke to share . . . with someone who would grin too and not bother to explain that the sign really meant "Wide Load" . . . with someone who wasn't a stranger.

The grader went away around the corner, fussing and fumbling out of sight around the hillside—and there it stopped. There was only the wind calling across the silence, bringing a chorus of bleating voices that must be sheep. Even the bulldozer had stopped, Simon realized. He supposed that the grader man too went back to town each night, leaving his grader parked somewhere off the road. He had just decided this when he heard a car start up and drive away: the sober-faced, whiskery driver going home. When the sound of the car had faded, Simon went walking along the road.

He didn't have to go very far. As he followed the road around the mountain's curve, the grader soon came in sight, tucked safely into the mouth of a shallow gully. Anyone driving past at night would hardly even see it. Simon admired its rakish leanness and the sober way it wore its cabin roof. It had none of the blunt, hard strength of the bulldozer.

He walked back looking at wheel-tracks in the gravel it had spread, and the ridge in the center of the road that marked the end of the blade. In one of the wheel-tracks was a little gray-green shape with arms and legs stretched out like a swimmer's. He bent over it: a small green swimmer from the swamp. The grader had run over a frog.

The little cries of a thousand frogs came shrilling from

the swamp. Simon picked this one up by a leg and carried it there. Killed on the road . . . the swamp could have it back. He placed it in the midst of a bull grass tussock and drew the grass together above it. When he stood up, something was there. Golden eyes, watching him. He knew what it was.

The Potkoorok rose up slowly, water sliding off its green skin while it watched the boy. It stood about two feet tall with its webbed feet hidden in the swamp and its legs bent at the knee. Its golden eyes were old like the eyes of lizards, and its froglike face was sad for the dead frog. Because it was the face of a joker, it looked comical with the wide mouth turned down. The Potkoorok had played its tricks on fishermen, men, and boys, in the days of the dark people; and in earlier times that the dark tribes had forgotten. It knew boys. For every ripple that glinted on the swamp, the Potkoorok had known ten boys; but never one who returned a dead frog so gently to the swamp. It spoke to him with a sound like lapping water.

"The yellow machine will follow where the water runs after the storm. The yellow machine is too much trouble."

It turned its head on its squat neck, looking at the boy from one old eye and then the other. While the boy still stood unable to move, the round green body of the Pot-koorok slipped back into the water.

It had gone. Simon still couldn't move. He had not expected anything so froglike or so human. He had not expected the swamp-creature at all—not standing there in broad daylight, only as a green shadow turning in the water. And he had never even thought of it speaking. He listened again to the gurgling voice and heard the words. They didn't make sense, and yet there was a feeling of solemn importance about them.

A hill caught him in its slanting shadow, and the swamp darkened. Simon saw that it was time to go. The wind had fallen, and Pet had eaten all the grass within reach. He managed to climb into her saddle from the log while clutching the reins, having no thought to spare for being nervous. He forgot his stick, but it didn't matter. Pet was going home; sometimes she even broke into a rough trot.

"After *what* storm?" said Simon.

There was no sign of any storm; just the dry, clear stillness after wind and the loud bleatings of sheep. The swamp-creature was tricking him again—it must think he was stupid to go on falling for its tricks every time. But— seeing it—! He felt alive with the excitement of seeing it.

Then he saw the sheep. Their bleating was so loud that at last he noticed it and looked. A mob of them was just crossing the creek at the mouth of the gully; Charlie had brought them in from that other paddock. He was coming behind them slowly on Surprise, and here and there darted the dogs. Simon watched them trail slowly out of sight behind the home ridge. By the time he reached the house he was surprised to find Charlie already there, un-saddling. When he saw Simon's face he grinned in a satis-fied way.

"Came home for a cup and left the dogs to carry on," he said. "You'll see them if you look down on the flat."

Simon went across to the fence and looked down. The sheep were a gray-white moving stream at the foot of the wooded ridge, and the dogs were working hard around the edge of it, turning the sheep up the ridge toward Wongadilla's half of the forest. Charlie came and watched too, full of pride in his dogs. When the sheep began to straggle upward, he whistled. The dogs left them and came like arrows, racing up the steep home ridge with little yelps.

Simon took his lunch things into the kitchen.

"*There* you are," said Edie. "You could do with a cup, then. How was the swamp?"

"The grader killed a frog," said Simon. It was all he could tell about the swamp that Edie might understand.

"It did?" said Edie. "We'll be having a storm, then."

"A *storm?*" Simon was staring.

"It's just an old saying. If you kill a frog, it'll call up a storm."

"*Whose* old saying?" Simon demanded.

"Well . . . I suppose it was the Aborigines. You'd better ask Charlie."

"We *can't* have a storm after all that wind," said Simon crossly, and stalked outside to do his share of holding things and passing things.

Charlie showed him how to let Pet go and feed her with chaff. The sky was a pale clear blue with a shine to it like the chime of a bell. The tops of eastern hills still wore sunlight, and the air had the sharp bite of late winter.

"Did you bring the sheep back in case of a storm?" asked Simon.

"Eh?" said Charlie. "Storm? We won't get a storm after that wind. Now the fence is fixed, it's time this paddock had a bit of use, that's all." He shook his head a little, and Simon had an annoyed feeling that he was laughing inside, silently. "Sheep have to get used to storms," he said.

The sky was sugared with stars when Simon went to bed. He woke to wildness and pounding and blue and white flashes. The storm had come. He woke, sitting up in protest—he had never heard rain pounding on an iron roof before. The sound almost drowned the angrier noise of thunder. Hard gusts of wind pushed in through the window and out again like a fist. Sheet lightning sketched the room in strong, clear lines: the curtains flying at the window, the opening door, and Edie's face appearing there.

"All right, Simey? Just a bit of a storm, it won't last. I'll shut your window." She came across and closed it. "A bit of a surprise, this, eh? You'll see the river up in the morning."

In an old gray gown and with her hair tousled Edie looked somehow like a very young child. He didn't mind much when she gave his blankets a tug and patted them quickly to see if they were wet. Then she went away on her round of the windows.

Simon lay listening to the thunder and the hammers of the rain. They had their storm, then, the swamp-thing

46

and the frog, and it sounded as if the water would flow all right. Would the yellow machine follow? He heard the veranda door close as Edie went back to bed. He couldn't possibly go to sleep. The pine tree whined and whimpered. The smack of wind made the house tremble, and after every lightning flash the picture of his room stayed photographed on his eyes in the darkness. Water-sounds were small and clear under the larger noises: the quick beat of drips on to the ground, the rippling of water along the roof-gutters, the glass-bell notes of water spilling from gutters into tanks. He could even hear it hissing on hot coals in the fireplace.

He sat up again. If he could hear that, then the rain must be stopping. He couldn't have heard it ten minutes ago. He eased the window up again and put his head out.

Black shapes of trees sprang up and vanished. Thunder scolded. The rain was quite light when you heard it on the grass instead of on the roof. There were stars again, wide fields of them between black flying clouds. It was still windy up there, but down here there were only gusts to shake splattering showers out of the trees. . . . There was moonlight! The air was so clear that wetness had a cold white shine from the moonlight. . . . There were black shadows flying, bigger than birds. . . .

The black shadows were leaping from tree to tree, from high to low. Arms and legs were spread, straggling beards floated. They called to each other in high, wild voices above and around the house. Excitement ran prickling along Simon's veins. He tumbled silently out of bed, rolled up his pajama legs, pulled on shorts and a raincoat and tennis shoes, climbed out of the window, and closed it down except for a space where he could fit his fingers. He was outside in the wet moonlight with black shadows leaping and calling overhead.

He went quietly toward the shed, and when he was nearer that than the house spoke softly to the dogs. Just as well he had been helping Charlie feed them; they only whimpered a bit when he told them to be quiet, and then he was past.

His shoes were wet and clammy-cold already. The rain had stopped, but the trees shook down drops that rattled on his raincoat and freckled his face with cold. The storm flashed and rumbled farther away, but here were only the calls of the flitting shadows and the water-noises—the *cluck* and *chinkle* of the creek down there in the gully; the louder rush and babble of the river; the quiet mutter of water running over the ground and sopping into his shoes, and somewhere the singing of water over high rocks.

Simon went running through the wet, shining white world, up the ridge past the head of the gully and then west to the swamp—seeing brambles and rocks and logs just in time to jump over them or swerve aside—somehow never falling—lifted and hurried along by the wet, magic night. He went running right into the swamp before he heard another sound than water-noises, and then he stopped, up to his ankles in the swamp. The song of frogs went creaking and hiccuping up to the moon, and beyond the swamp was a clank and rattle of metal.

The road came out of a blackness of trees, water running down in a sheet because the mountain poured it off too fast for the gutters to carry it away. Into the moonlight came the grader as if the water carried it, clanking along slow and majestic like a lanky skeleton ship. But all around it there was a flurry of shadows, calling and crying as they had in the trees. Wispy arms waved, sticklike knees bent, shadowy beards tossed. They crowded the cabin and rode on the blade and clustered along its sides, the Turongs carrying the grader.

The boy stared, breathing hard. When the grader reached the turn, it left the road and came on down to the swamp, slow and majestic like a battleship, but clanking as it was carried along by the crowd of dancing shadows. More of them came down from the trees, calling in windy voices. The grader reached the deep end of the swamp, and there the Potkoorok was waiting.

Into the shallows while frogs were shrieking; on while the wheels sank deeper and the blade dipped under. A lurch, a slow roll, a sinking down of the cabin roof; dark water heaving under the moon—and the grader was gone. The Turongs rustled and stamped and jigged, the Potkoorok leaped and chuckled. The boy ran away, slopping through the swamp while the frogs shrieked.

He wanted to yell with delight or terror. He wanted to dance with the stamping, jigging, hopping crowd—if only he hadn't dreaded that they might come near. There was nothing to do but run. He splashed through runnels and

49

stumbled over bushes while the cries died away behind. The wet, magic night no longer held him up, and once he fell over. That made him realize that the moon was now hidden and he was running in the dark. A few last rags of cloud had blown across just as he left the swamp.

He would have to stop being stupid. He stood still and listened to the watery night. He remembered he should be walking across a gradual slope with a steep rise on the right and the ridge running down to the left. The easier slope of the ridge should guide him to the house, even if the moon didn't come out again soon—and it would, of course. It wasn't even dark, now that he looked, except for the close-looming blackness of the mountain. In the gray light of stars and cloudy moon he could see darker shapes ahead.

He squelched on. A faint gray shine was the wet wood of a fallen branch; he walked carefully around it. There was a tree close by in the blackness of the hillside. He *felt* its closeness and found it by putting out a hand and touching wet bark. Branches stirred, and drops pelted on his raincoat. The darkness and the slow groping made him colder.

Something moved; he felt it close to him. Invisible against the mountain, something big and solid moved a little. Simon stood still and listened: no snort from the horses, no breathing, no twitch of ear or tail. He listened as he had not known he could, listened with every inch of his skin: he heard nothing. No pumping heart, no quietly streaming blood. Only the unhearable sound of earth taking a weight, only the universe shifting to balance a small movement. He wanted to put out a hand to discover what moved close by—but the dark places in his mind told his hand to be still, as they told his heart to beat quietly.

The moon's edge lifted from the cloud; there was soft polished light, and he saw a crooked shape. About a yard away—leaning forward—a hard, craggy, blunt-muzzled head and the smallest, most secret movement of a limb. Something without heart or blood, the living earth in a squat and solid shape, reached very secretly, a very little, for Simon.

He wasted no energy to yell or gasp. His stretched nerves twanged, he shot ten feet in one leap and kept on running. Away behind him something cried out savagely in anger—*Nga-a-a!* The wild, fierce cry laid its echo like a trail along the mountain. The dogs barked for a moment and were silent. Simon raced, crept in among them and crouched there, and the dogs whimpered, and he whimpered with them. They listened together and peered into the moonlight. Silence. Nothing moved on the ridge.

After a time Simon whispered shaky words of comfort to the dogs and forced himself to go the little way to the house. He raised the window and climbed in, pulled off his wet shoes and dropped them outside and shut the window. He tore off coat and shorts and plunged into bed.

The cooling hot-water bag felt scorching, he was so cold. He tried not to shake the bed by shivering. It was very quiet; no sound at all except the creek and the river. Moonlight lay gently on his red·felt mat, and only the pine

51

tree whispered against the stars.

It was the moon coming out like that, he decided. He was excited by those crazy, wonderful, weird creatures at the swamp; and then groping through the dark, and the moon coming out, and an owl or something screeching. He had seen some rock and imagined the horror. And thinking this he fell into exhausted sleep.

He didn't hear the sound that woke Charlie and brought him to the window: the shrill, terrified bleating of a sheep.

4

SIMON WOKE EARLY and suddenly, remembering his
nightmare as he woke. The whole night might almost
have been a dream, storm and all. It was a bright, fresh
morning, the creek and the river making hardly more
noise than usual by now. There were only frail wisps of
vapor rising from fence posts and logs to prove there had
been a storm; and Simon's wet raincoat under the bed,
and his soggy tennis shoes outside the window.

He dressed, wondering if anything at all had really
happened at the swamp in the night or if he had imagined
that wild and wonderful scene as well as the other. He
wished, with a rush of loneliness and longing, that he
could talk to someone about it and ask if he were going
mad. Not Charlie or Edie, of course; he still couldn't even
say "Charlie" or "Edie," and wondered hopelessly if he
ever would. He was sure that at his first word about the
swamp-creature and the sticklike shadows Edie would

want to tuck him up with a hot-water bottle. Charlie would say, in that serious way that meant Charlie was laughing inside, that there were a lot of shadows about in the moonlight. . . . And so there were. . . .

He went to the kitchen, where Charlie and Edie had just finished breakfast and were talking seriously.

". . . didn't like the sound of it," Charlie was saying. "Have to have a look around today—" He broke off as Simon appeared in the doorway and gave him one of those quick, direct looks. Edie got up to break an egg into the pan.

"*There* you are, then," said Charlie, in pleased surprise. "Turning into a cocky, eh? Pull up a chair, mate. You're a useful bloke to have around, predicting storms out of the blue. Better than the weatherman."

"Did you get back to sleep?" asked Edie, spooning melted butter over the egg.

"Old sheep didn't disturb you?" added Charlie.

Simon was considering this question, which he didn't understand, when the dogs began to bark and yell. The next minute a voice called from the back door.

"Anyone home?"

Charlie swiveled his chair around to go to the door. It opened, and there stood a thin, stooped man with a long face and a bristly chin. Simon gripped the edge of the table—it was the driver of the grader.

"Morning, mate," said Charlie formally. "What can I do for you?"

The driver looked all around the kitchen, nodded to

Simon, looked around the kitchen again, and at last said, "You wouldn't happen to have seen a grader about, would you?"

Charlie answered gravely. "Can't say we have."

"You didn't happen to hear anything like a grader going by? Say, between four last night and seven this morning?"

Charlie and Edie shook their heads. Edie spooned more butter over Simon's egg. Charlie said, with polite concern, "What, lost a grader, have you?" The kitchen was full of their silent, impish laughter. Simon almost heard it. He too was full of silent laughter, for it seemed that he wasn't mad after all. The grader was gone; the shadows that glided from tree to tree and danced by the swamp were real.

The grader-man too could hear the silent laughter and had been expecting it. He looked at the floor, at the table, at the ceiling, at the window, anywhere except at Charlie. "Could've sworn I left the brake on," he confessed.

"You could do with a cup," said Charlie, reaching for the teapot. "Pull up a chair . . . Milk and sugar if you want it . . . Where did you leave her?"

"Half a mile up from the turn by your swamp."

"You never left her in the gully mouth?"

The driver shuffled his feet. "It was dry as chips after the wind. I'm certain I left the brake on." He took a deep draft of tea and made another confession. "They'll be fit to be tied when they find out. There'll be a fine old fuss."

"We'll have to find her, then," said Charlie kindly. "No tracks, of course?"

The driver shook his head. "All washed out."

"The wash should be as good as tracks. We'll get going as soon as you've had your tea—I've got a bit extra to do today myself. Coming, young feller?"

"He'll want his breakfast first," said Edie firmly. "He'll catch you up."

The driver finished his tea and followed Charlie outside, complaining as he went about the unfairness of things. "The brake was on and the blade was down, only they won't believe me. There'd be no moving her—short of a flood—"

"A man can't expect a storm out of a clear sky," Charlie consoled him, shutting the door.

While he ate his breakfast, Simon heard the station wagon drive out of the shed and away down the ridge. "We can saddle Pet," Edie told him. "You can get there nearly as soon, across the paddock."

He was feeling alive with the joy of knowing that his stick-shadows were real. "On *Pet?*" he said cheekily.

Edie's withered-petal face grew warm with delight. "If you're in a hurry, you can walk," she said, dropping bread into the toaster.

He did walk, on the plea of getting a ride in the station wagon later. "Can—can I have an apple?" he managed to ask at the last minute.

Edie gave him one, and then another one for later.

Simon succeeded in saying "Thanks" and erupted from the kitchen feeling embarrassed but successful.

He went running up the ridge to the point where he had to turn off the track to the left along the mountain. There he slowed down suddenly. It must have been somewhere here. . . . He went slowly, looking for the rock or stump or bush that had seemed so horrifying in the sudden moonlight. He couldn't find one.

"Things always look wrong and different at night," he reminded himself, and went running on again to the swamp.

At the edge where he had gone splashing in last night he stopped again to look. *This* was better. This he could remember clearly, just as it had looked in the moonlight. There were the trees out of whose shadows the grader had come into sight, with the spindly creatures clustered over it and dancing round. The magic of it reached out and took him again. There must have been hundreds of them, and more coming down from the trees all the time, and still more traveling to the swamp springing from tree to tree. Creatures of the trees—what had they to do with the swamp-creature and the frog? Why was the yellow machine a trouble to *them?* You'd think tree-things would have picked on the bulldozer; that was a yellow machine, too, and surely more of a trouble to tree-creatures.

Simon went down to the deep end of the swamp and peered into the water. There wasn't a sign. The hole couldn't be deep enough to hide a whole grader! They must have moved it again. He threw one of Edie's apples into the water for the swamp-creature and went across soft muddy soil to the road.

The grader's work had all been washed away, and water had cut fresh grooves in the surface of the road. Simon went along it again until he could see the place where the grader had been parked; Charlie's station wagon was parked there now. He and the driver would have climbed down the mountainside to see if the grader had been washed over there. Simon went back toward the swamp.

There was some commotion in the scrub above it. Out of the trees came a scatter of sheep, small hooves pelting as if something were after them. They swung east along the mountain and went racing back toward the home ridge. Simon looked after them thoughtfully, hesitated for a minute, then went up the mountain into the scrub.

The terraces between the roots were soft and squashy to walk on after the storm. He was pelted at once with a heavy shower of twigs, and remembered that the bulldozer had been covered in twigs and sticks on a night of little wind. Small paws went scuttling everywhere among the leaves, and something big that couldn't be seen came bounding toward him with heavy thumps until at last he had to dodge aside. Since there was really nothing there, this made him feel foolish.

"You want to watch it!" he called loudly.

A few more twigs hit him. The running paws scampered by. He caught a glimpse of movement at the edge of his vision, but when he turned his head there was nothing there. Wherever he looked there was movement in some other direction.

When this had happened three or four times, Simon stood quiet and looked steadily ahead. After a while, from the corners of his eyes, he saw three gray shadows with straggling beards, scuttling like spiders around the trunks of trees.

"Caught you!" he crowed, pointing—and was pelted with twigs again. "Anyhow," he shouted, "you got the wrong machine!"

There was utter stillness in the scrub. Delighted with himself, Simon went running down the root terraces into the sunlight. The song of frogs lay over the swamp. At the far end, sitting on the bank with its legs in the water, sat the green-skinned, golden-eyed swamp-creature eating an apple.

Simon stood still while excitement fluttered in his veins. The swamp-thing stayed peacefully where it was. Simon took the second apple from his pocket and went slowly to the bank and sat down. The swamp-creature gave him a comical look. They sat side by side on the bank, both chewing apples and Simon swelling with delight. After a while he ventured to speak.

"What's your name?" It was a stupid thing to say to a swamp-thing, but how else could you start?

The swamp-creature made a sound like the calling of frogs.

"Eh?" said Simon.

The creature made the sound again: "Potkoorok."

"Is that your own name? Or is it what you are?"

"That is my name that I am," said the creature, a little grandly. "You are Boy. I am Potkoorok." It put the last bit of apple into its froglike mouth and crunched away. Juice ran out of the corners of its mouth. "Good," it said, turning its head toward Simon.

"Pot-koo-rok," said Simon. The creature chuckled. "And what are *they*? The ones in the trees?"

"Turongs. Tu-rongs. Their name that they are is Tu-rongs." It was watching Simon with sly attention.

"Turongs," repeated Simon thoughtfully. "*Hey!*"

He had lost his apple. A green hand with flattened webbed fingers had plucked it lightly from his own hand while he spoke. The Potkoorok chuckled with glee and munched the remains of the apple. Simon supposed that if you wanted to be friends with it you would have to put up with that sort of thing.

"There's a lot more Turongs up there now, aren't there?" he said. "Did they come from the other scrub when the trees were cut down?" The Potkoorok's wide mouth turned down, and it looked at him sadly. "Why do they throw sticks and chase the sheep? *We* didn't cut down their trees."

"They play jokes," said the Potkoorok reproachfully. "On hunters—not so good as fishermen. They can't help it; they are Turongs, not Potkooroks. They play jokes good enough for hunters. If there are no hunters, what can they do? They play tricks on sheep."

"*You* played a trick on *them* last night," said Simon. "You made them pinch the wrong machine."

"No trick. The Turongs want to sink the wrong machine. It is wrong for them too. The yellow machine is a wrong trouble, killing frogs and trees."

"But that was two different machines! This one killed the frog, the other one killed the trees. The Turongs wanted to get rid of the other one."

The Potkoorok gave him an offended look. "The Turongs brought the yellow machine," it said huffily.

"Both of them were yellow! You just wait—the other one will go on killing trees on the mountain."

The Potkoorok turned its golden eyes along the mountain and looked far off. "The Boy tricks the Potkoorok," it said dryly. "I see no yellow machine on the mountain."

As it happened, the bulldozer was not working that morning, so Simon was not able to prove his point. In any case, the Potkoorok seemed upset, and that was a bad way to begin a friendship. He set out to soothe its ruffled feelings.

"What happened to the machine, anyhow? I looked in the water and it's gone. You can't see anything at all."

This was evidently the right thing to say, for the creature chuckled like the lapping of water. "You can't see anything at all? You look now," it said.

Simon stood up and looked into the pool. Clearly, through the brown water, he could see a yellow shape: a wheel, and part of a frame. While he was looking, the water grew dark again. Nothing showed.

"Hey!" said Simon. "Would you believe that?"

The Potkoorok was chuckling away when the sound of a motor came from the road. Still chuckling and without a splash, the creature slid into the water and was gone. Simon was almost relieved. It had been a tremendous excitement, but a strain too. He wanted time to think about it and grow used to it.

He guessed that the motor would be Charlie's, driving home after the search had been given up, so he went to the bend of the road to wait for it. But it was not the station wagon that came around the curve of the mountain. It was a blue car, much newer and smarter, driven by a stocky young man wearing a navy singlet. He stopped the car when he saw Simon and leaned through the window to speak.

"Nice day after the storm. . . . Haven't seen a bull-dozer about, have you?"

It was the driver of the bulldozer, and he too was looking for his machine.

5

THE DISAPPEARANCE of the bulldozer as well as the grader caused a fuss that took up the rest of that day. It began at the telephone in Charlie's small study where drivers rang up their bosses and the police, and the police rang up other police and neighbors and townspeople to help in the search. Edie was kept busy making tea for them and listening to their telephone conversations.

From there the fuss spread all around Wongadilla. Cars nosed along roads and tracks, four-wheel-drive vehicles charged into gullies; the whining and grinding of their motors hung round the hills all day. There were constant meetings between men who exchanged theories, agreed with each other, massaged their heads, and lapsed into puzzled silence. Only the grader man was sure of anything, and he grew more certain every moment that the brake of the grader had been fully on.

There were times when Simon, following them about,

wondered whether he ought to tell about the grader. But he was sure they would not believe him if he did and somehow just as sure that people should not interfere with the creatures of the country. Besides, he had no idea what could have happened to the bulldozer. Perhaps, after he had run home last night, the wild crowd of Turongs had gone on across the mountain and carried off the bulldozer too. Yet he didn't believe this. The Potkoorok would have known and boasted about it, instead of being huffy when he mentioned two machines.

Late in the afternoon Charlie extricated himself and Simon from the search, telling the searchers to help themselves to the telephone if they needed it and that he had to check up on some sheep. By that time the searchers were ready to give up in any case and began to drive away. The final theory was that thieves or practical jokers had driven the two machines off last night, unheard in the storm, and that the police must look for them miles away from Wongadilla.

Simon and Charlie came into the kitchen where Edie was already pouring their tea. She looked at Charlie with a questioning face. "Not a sign," he told her. "They'd have to be *somewhere*, they couldn't vanish."

"It won't do any good," said Edie in a vexed way, pushing the sugar basin toward him. "There'll be another bulldozer up there inside a week."

"Anyhow, this one's nowhere on Wongadilla. They reckon it's been stolen, and I'd say they're right. A wasted day, and too late to get around the sheep tonight—best I can do is have a look at their camp. I wish these machine men could look after their own stock. Eh, Simey?"

Simon didn't really hear. He was listening, at last, to the silence with its clear, frail sounds. He was tired of interruptions and strangers and excitement. Now he wanted to be alone with the silence and the windy heights of Wongadilla, letting them restore to him the small old creatures of the land. Later, though he sat between Charlie and Edie, he was alone with the fire; and he thought of the Potkoorok stealing his apple and smiled and hugged himself. Then he was alone between the white walls of his room, hearing the pine whisper and a fox call: and he thought of spidery gray shadows climbing around trunks. He went to sleep thinking of the Turongs' dance and woke deciding to spend the day alone on the mountain.

Charlie was going to muster the sheep and look them over, as he had meant to do yesterday. "I could do with a hand," he told Simon, "that's if you've got nothing better to do." When Simon stammered that he thought he might go and look at the place where the bulldozer had been, Charlie said quickly, "That's right, you look around while you've got the chance. You wouldn't want to go through the fence, of course—one of those trees could make a mess of you if it happened to fall on you." He helped Simon to catch Pet while Edie cut lunch for them both, and watched Simon ride off alone without seeming to mind at all. He only shouted after him: "If you see any sheep, send 'em down!" And Simon waved in reply and then forgot. Perhaps a cicada feels as Simon did when it crawls out of the earth in its tight shell.

He rode first to the foot of the steepest slope and reined in near the fence; the screen of forest had been cleared from there, and he could see what the bulldozer had done. Before it disappeared, it had flattened about half the forest on that side of the fence. No one was working there today.

Someone would come and finish the job, he supposed. Someone would load and cart away the trimmed logs and perhaps burn the others. Grass would grow in time, and bracken and a few new trees. Then it would look like any other ridge. Now it looked barer and uglier than the rocks that rose above it at the end of the mountain.

Standing in the stirrups and switching at Pet's rump with his stick, he forced her up the trail that had frightened him that first time. Whenever the trail turned and she was faced with the need to clamber higher, Pet stopped dead until Simon shouted and switched. They came at last to the ledge, and he got off and tethered her where Charlie had. He walked to the fence and looked down, as he had that other day. There was no place down there to hide a bulldozer except in the forest itself; even the Turongs couldn't have done it. The bulldozer must have gone out by the way it came in, as the searchers had said. He went back to the ledge and looked down at Wongadilla.

There it was, plunging down, with blue heights swinging up beyond. There was the glinting green of the swamp, and the white shoebox house. Some tiny sheep were collected on the flat; he could hear Charlie's shouts and the answering yelps of the dogs. Next time, he thought, he would have to give Charlie a hand—when he had sorted out the things he wanted to think about.

Now it must be nearly "time for a cup." He took an apple from his lunch bag: Edie had given him two. Simon suddenly knew that Edie would always give him two apples, since yesterday when he had asked for one. He took the apple across the steep slope to that little gully where he had been before; last time he had climbed into it from high up the mountain, and he had climbed out again at about this level.

It was very quiet and alone in there, just as he remembered. He could look down the gully over Wongadilla, but no one there would see him, leaning back against the side like this. He sat there eating his apple and feeling the strength of the mountain surging behind him. He felt the earth rolling on its way through the sky, and rocks and trees clinging to it, and seas and the strands of rivers pressed to it, and flying birds caught in its net of air. And though he didn't know what the Potkoorok and the Turongs were, still he knew they were part of the earth and this mountain. People might come and go, he thought, but those others belonged here; and he thought they had belonged here always. There was something old and innocent in the way the Turongs danced and in the sly teasing of the Potkoorok. There was something that didn't care—

something free and old like the mountain and elusive like the blue shadows of distance. Simon could not have explained it, but he knew it.

His breath came quicker when he faced the question of what these old creatures *were*. For the only words that came to him were "elf" and "magic"—and surely those meant something different? He put the question away again and thought of the Turongs: "If there are no hunters, what can they do? They play tricks on sheep." Once they had played their tricks on dark-skinned hunters, he thought; and they had lived in a wide world of forests instead of fleeing from one small scrap to the next. . . .

BRENT, said the gully silently.

Simon frowned. No one could have spoken his name up here. Nothing interrupted the silence. He went back to his thoughts.

BRENT, said the gully.

Simon shifted in an irritated way. He looked and saw his name scratched on a small rock—he must have been seeing it for some time without really seeing. It made him jump at first, until he remembered scratching it there himself the other time he was here. He must be sitting in almost the same spot as he was that day.

BRENT, said the gully, speaking urgently. He shrugged, trying to forget it. He frowned and looked about, then sat up straight, frowning again.

Where was SIMON?

He had scratched both names, on two rocks, side by

side so that they made his whole name, SIMON BRENT. Here was BRENT; where was SIMON?

He began to look around, puzzled: it had been a big rock, very big, leaning against the wall of the gully with the smaller rock on its other side. He remembered quite well. The blue-green lichen in which he scratched his name had been bigger, too; it had caught his eye first and started him off with his name-scratching. He had made the first name so big that there was no room left for the second. Idly, not really thinking much about it, he had looked for a place to scratch the second name and noticed the small rock with a smaller lichen. They had stood close, side by side, and made his whole name between them, even though the second name was smaller.

So where was SIMON?

"That's mad!" he said angrily, and got up to search. No one could have moved a big rock like that! Even in the storm, even a *torrent* of water rushing down couldn't have moved it . . . but perhaps it might have moved the smaller rock? Perhaps he wasn't in the same place at all but a little further down the gully? He went to examine the smaller rock.

He grasped it and wrenched at it, but it stayed firm. It was set in the earth; ferns and grass stood around its base and nothing had disturbed them. . . . But there were crushed ferns and grass and smeared moss in a patch between the small rock and the gully wall. It didn't look as though a great rock had been torn from the ground where it belonged—but something very heavy *had* been moved.

He looked for more crushed ferns and moss and saw a patch on rocks six feet higher up the gully. From there he saw, higher still, a deep groove plowed into soft soil; and beyond that a scraped muddy mark on a flat rock. From sign to sign, he traced a trail up the gully between walls that grew steeper and closer as he went.

Up the gully!

"It's mad!" cried Simon angrily again.

Then he hit on a solution to the mystery and wondered why he hadn't thought of it before. The Turongs, of course. He couldn't guess why or how they had moved a great boulder up this little gully, but they must have done it; and who knew how or why the Turongs did anything? Greatly relieved he came to a sharp elbow in the gully and stopped.

Ahead, he could see, the gully was choked with blackberry. In front of this screen, leaning against the wall of the gully, was a great unevenly shaped boulder that called to him silently: SIMON. He took a step toward it—and stopped again.

It had a queer crouching shape that looked as if it were pressing itself against the side of the gully, hiding its face. It was stone, dark with age and heavy and still as stone; if you saw it suddenly in the moonlight, would it move, a very little and very slowly, toward you? Simon began to back carefully away, watching it. That was not a blunt muzzle pressed against the rock; it was only stone. That cavity was not an eye full of darkness; it saw nothing. He backed away around the elbow of the gully, then turned and began to scurry down.

When he came to the stone marked BRENT, he did not climb out of the gully but hurried past. He didn't want the slow trouble of getting Pet down the mountain; he wanted to reach the Potkoorok. The little gully shallowed and widened, merging into the mountain's broad lap. Just inside its mouth he came on something very ugly: a sheepskin, mangled and torn, with flies buzzing about it and small hooves still attached. The hooves were crushed and flattened as if something heavy had smashed them. He took his eyes away from it with a shiver and began running hard along the mountain.

When he got to the swamp, there was no sign of the swamp-creature. He had no idea how to summon it and no apple to offer it. He tried calling.

"Potkoorok!"

No sign. Of course it wouldn't come when it knew he wanted it; it would hide and try to surprise him. But he called again urgently:

"Potkoorok!"

When it didn't come, he grew desperate and shouted a mixture of pleading and command: "I gave you apples— I didn't tell about the grader—I picked up the frog—I *need* you! Come!"

It came out of the water at his feet and sat on a tuft of bull grass, looking slightly offended as if Simon's manners displeased it; but when it saw that he was desperately serious, it grew uneasy instead.

"Listen!" said Simon, trying to breathe and talk evenly and slowly. "Up there on the mountain—there's a thing —a big stone. Did the Turongs move it?"

The Potkoorok stiffened. It spoke sternly. "They leave it alone. It doesn't belong here. It is the Nargun."

"Go on," Simon demanded. "Does it move by itself, then? Is it another one—like you? Is it good?"

"Good?" said the Potkoorok. "What is good? It is the Nargun. It came from a long way south. It should go back."

"Does it—hurt things? Would it—kill a sheep?"

The Potkoorok blinked its old-looking eyes and turned its head away. It scooped up a water-spider in its webbed fingers and held it up with a coaxing smile for Simon to admire.

"Would it hurt a person?" Simon persisted.

The Potkoorok gave him a huffy look and slipped off the tuft of grass into the water. It was gone.

Simon stood helpless. He thought he had met the Nargun by moonlight, standing heavy and cold and still. He thought it had cried after him savagely when he ran and hid with the whimpering dogs. But he didn't know, and there was no one else he could ask. He only knew that a great heavy stone had been moved up the small gully from the place where it had been; and that in the mouth of the gully lay the crushed remains of a sheep. He didn't know what to do.

From down in the big gully where the creek ran came

Charlie's voice shouting to the dogs: "Go back, Tess—back! Nipper! Keep out!" A dog yelped excitedly, and a sheep bleated. Simon ran again, past the swamp and the head of the gully, along the ridge till he could see Charlie and the sheep below. He plunged into the gully.

"*Charlie!*" he shouted, running down the ridge. He gulped for breath and shouted again. "Charlie! *Charlie!*"

Charlie wheeled his horse and came at the creek. The dogs looked back and hesitated.

"Charlie— Charlie—"

All in a minute, Surprise was hitched to a stump and Charlie was running up the ridge. Edie appeared on the opposite ridge near the house, and stood there. The sheep scattered. The dogs watched them uncertainly and followed Charlie up the ridge looking ashamed and foolish.

"All right, mate, what's up?" said Charlie. "Come on, now, you're all right. What's up, Simey? Snake bite you?"

Simon shook his head, fighting for breath and for words to say. Charlie waved reassuringly to Edie and sat Simon down on a log. The dogs came close and licked his knees.

"You need a cup," said Charlie, and went striding down to Surprise. He came back with a mug half full of tea and said, "There, get that down."

Simon gulped cold air and hot tea in turns, still trying to find something to say. At last he began shakily: "I'm not mad—"

Charlie sat down on the log beside him. "Never knew anyone saner," he said firmly.

Simon tried again. "You've lost a sheep."

"Thought so," said Charlie, nodding. "Old ewe. Always asking for trouble, never would stick with the mob. What got her?"

"The Nargun, I think—a great thing up the mountain —it's made of *stone*, but the Potkoorok says it's a Nargun! I nearly ran into it, I think, the night they put the grader in the swamp—" He wanted to stop the words that were coming out wildly, for now Charlie would surely think he was mad, but he couldn't stop them. "I wrote my *name* on it, I didn't *know*. And the hooves are all crushed, crushed flat—" He stopped at last, shaking, his head well down so that he needn't face Charlie's serious, silent laughter.

"I never heard of a Nargun," said Charlie, "but the Potkoorok ought to know. So they put the grader in the swamp, did they? Should've thought of that, I suppose."

At this Simon turned his face against the faded blue sleeve of Charlie's shirt. After a minute he said, "Pet's up the mountain. I left her there."

"Surprise can take us both up when you've done with that tea," said Charlie. "As far as the steep bit, anyway. You're not too solid, and I'm a skinny old bag of bones, so we'll just make one decent load for him. . . . Potkoorok scare you?"

"Heck, no," said Simon. "*It's* all right. So are the Turongs."

Charlie nodded. "Edie and I used to like 'em when we were kids, so we thought you would too. We'd have

74

warned you, only you'd have thought we were putting you on. Besides, we didn't know if you'd see them; not many people do."

"Do other places have them? Or is it only Wongadilla?"

"I don't know about that, boy—*I* never heard of any others. Edie and I used to talk sometimes: whatever there was before white men came, like elves and spirits and that, they must live *somewhere* when you come to think about it. *We* only know the Wongadilla ones, because they've always been here and we happened to come across them when we were kids. I reckon most people never even dream of 'em. Never expected you to see 'em either, at least not for a good while yet. Sure they didn't scare you?"

Simon was indignant. "They're *great!* Anyhow, you couldn't have Wongadilla without them. I reckon they're part of it, like—like the gully."

"*You're* all right, then. That's about what Edie and I always reckoned."

"It's this Nargun. The Potkoorok says the others won't go near it and it came from a long way off and it ought to go away. And the sheep—" Simon took a breath and stopped.

"All right, keep cool," said Charlie. "We'll go and have a look at that now. I'll be surprised if any of the old things have any real harm in 'em, Nargun or not. The Potkoorok's a joker, you know. Still, we can't have you scared, and there's the sheep too. So we'll just see if Surprise'll let us both on board when we bring him up out of

the gully, and then you can tell me about it from the beginning as we go. You didn't make a very good job of it
last time."

Simon went pink and grinned a bit. He was surprised
to find that a world with Charlie in it could be so normal
in spite of Turongs, Potkooroks, and even Narguns.

6

THE DOGS, Tess and Nipper, were sent back on duty to keep the sheep in the gully. Simon was perched behind the saddle on Surprise, clinging to Charlie's belt, and with Surprise's hindquarters springing under him in a way quite different from Pet's.

"Now," said Charlie, "we'll get this Nargun sorted out. Start again, Simey."

So Simon told about it in a few words at a time, speaking to Charlie's close and unfamiliar back. He told how, three days ago, he had scratched his name on the two rocks in the small gully and today had found the big one twenty yards or more higher up the gully; about the sheepskin with the crushed hooves, and what the Potkoorok had said; and even about his nightmare or fright after the storm. Whenever he stopped because the next bit seemed ridiculous, Charlie said, "M'p," and waited for him to go on. It didn't take long, and at the end they

77

bumped on in silence until Simon said, "What are we going to do?"

"Hard to say," said Charlie. "I haven't seen anything yet. But first we'll bring old Pet down and have some lunch."

When the track began to snake up the steep part, Charlie put Simon down near the fence and went on alone to bring Pet down. They hitched the two horses to the fence, unpacked both their lunches, and ate in the shade of a stringybark. After that they walked to the gully mouth.

It was easy to find the sheepskin again because of the flies. Charlie bent over it and swore in a disbelieving way while Simon stood by. He stood up again with a set face in which all the creases seemed to have been pressed deeper.

"Well I don't blame you for being a bit upset about that, mate." He shook his head. "Lord only knows what could've done that. . . . Fetch me some stones, Simey. We'll just put that by in case we need it." He picked up a stick to fold and roll the fleece while Simon collected a few big stones to cover it.

When that was done he followed Simon up the gully, frowning and silent. In its lower part, where the gully was broad and well-grassed with strong native grasses, there were no signs that Simon could see of anything heavy having moved. But soon the signs appeared—a gouge in wet soil, crushed moss, bruised grass, broken ferns, a long smear of mud on a rock—and Simon pointed to them one by one. Each time Charlie said, "M'p," and frowned.

They reached the small rock with BRENT in straggling

letters scratched in lichen, and here they paused while Charlie tried in vain to move the rock and examined the growth around it. Simon had to show where he had first come into the gully, where he had climbed out, where he had sat the second time, and to say if he was sure he hadn't got up and moved about between scratching the first name and the second. "M'p," said Charlie.

They left the place and went higher, Simon still pointing to signs along the way. The gully walls grew steeper and higher, water trickled between rocks, and they came to the angle like an elbow. Simon rounded it and stood looking at the great crouched stone. It was just stone. You couldn't say that cavity was like an eye—that it seemed to watch in a darkly knowing way, without understanding.

"That it?" said Charlie, and made a half move forward. But Simon happened to step in front of him. He looked at the rock for a while and then said, "M'p. Better get back to the horses."

Simon left it to Charlie to lead the way down, which he did in silence. At the mouth of the gully he stopped, his eyes on the little heap of stones around which the flies were still buzzing.

"Well, I don't know about any of that, Simey," he said. "That thing's stone if ever I saw stone. Solid. Nothing like the others. Maybe the Turongs have been playing games like they did with the grader, and maybe the Potkoorok was pulling your leg. We'll have to see what Edie thinks. But something's made a mess of the old ewe. It's a good thing we've got most of the sheep on the flat already. I'll send old Trig down to hold them while I get the rest across, and we'll have the lot back in the other paddock before dark."

"I'll help," said Simon.

"Good man! We'll have them out of the gully in time for a quick cup with Edie. We need it after that."

They rode down to the house so that Charlie could release old Trig from his chain and send him down the ridge to the sheep on the flat. Trig was excited and at first wanted to rush down the wrong side to Tess and Nipper; but Charlie got him launched in the right direction with a little yelling. It was odd to compare the happy eagerness of the dogs, the roughness of Charlie's shouted orders, and the warmth of pride on Charlie's face.

"Trig doesn't get out much these days," he explained to Simon. "Getting too old, like his boss. But there's nothing the old boy can't do, he's a wonder. *Go out, Trig,* you blockheaded old dingo! *Keep back,* there! Now, *stay!* They won't get past Trig, he'll hold them all night. *Stay, Trig,* you bludging old hound! You're getting as silly as a wet hen."

They left old Trig, watchful as a snake, holding the sheep on the flat in an angle of the fence. Charlie shouted to Edie, who had come out to look, that they would be in for a cup in a minute. Then he and Simon rode down the other side of the ridge into the big gully, where Charlie bullied Tess and Nipper into herding those sheep again. They took the sheep slowly down the gully, and at the turn Simon and Pet came into their own by standing firmly in the right place while the dogs raced and yelped and nipped. Charlie said that Simon and Pet had saved him twenty minutes. When these sheep had joined the others on the flat, they left the three dogs in charge and went back to the house for tea. Edie met them with a sudden, questioning look and cups of tea already poured.

There was a lot to explain to her, and Charlie explained in his own way. "Taking the stock back over the road," he said easily. "Something got the old crossbred ewe. Potkoorok says it was a Nargun, but it looks like a great stone to me. Simey can tell you about it later, he's the one that found her. Found the grader, too. It's in the swamp."

Edie threw her sudden look at Simon. "The grader, Simey? It's not deep enough to cover it," she said.

"It does if the Potkoorok wants it to," Simon explained.

She nodded. "You got your tennis shoes in a mess that night. Just as well you won't be needing them for tennis. They didn't upset you then, the old creatures?"

Simon looked at her: shaped like a hen, with a face made of dying petals, and knowing all the time that he'd been out after the storm. Still like a swamp, and giving him two apples ever after because he asked for one. His face warmed to a half-smile that passed to Edie's face like sunlight. "Edie," he said, and they all chuckled.

"That's all right, then," she said. "We'd have told you, only we didn't want to upset you. What's this about the ewe?"

Charlie pushed his cup back and stood up. "Not much

loss, poor old beast, and she asked for it. Simey'll tell you. I've got to get going—might be a bit late back."

When he had gone, Edie poured more tea into her cup and pushed a plate of biscuits toward Simon. "Potkooroks and Turongs wouldn't hurt," she said. "What frightened you, Simey? I heard you yelling."

So he told it all over again and watched uneasiness move over her face and turn into thought. "A Nargun . . . That's new. I never heard of one . . . but I don't think the Potkoorok would play that sort of trick. . . . Just as well to get the sheep away." She asked only one question. "Did you say it looked like stone? Or did you say it *is* a stone?"

Simon gripped the edge of the table. "It's a stone," he said on a deep breath, "a great enormous one. You can *tell* stone, you can see it's solid and heavy—and it's hard —and *grainy*—and *bumpy*—" But he couldn't say it had a muzzle, or dark cavities for eyes.

"Well," said Edie briskly, "if Charlie's going to be late, we've got our work cut out. He'll have to feed the dogs when he brings them home, but I can look after the cows and the rest. Dinner's about ready—we'll have it in front of the fire tonight, like a picnic. Would you just bring in some wood for the woodbox, Simey?"

"All right," said Simon. "And I'll fix Pet up."

The cows had come up from the creek early, perhaps disturbed by Tess and Nipper. Simon filled the woodbox, taking four trips to do it, while Edie milked. With her heavy body balanced on the stool and her thin legs gripping the pail, she looked like two different people milking the same cow. While she fed the cows, Simon unsaddled and fed Pet. He fed the hens and locked them in their run while Edie went inside to light the fire.

By the time Charlie came home, the fire was well alight, its soft crunchings and spittings pleasant to hear. The picnic dinner was set in front of it, and Edie was measuring a length of blue knitting against Simon's arm.

During dinner Charlie told Simon how he and Edie had first met the Potkoorok when they were children: it had tipped them out of a homemade canoe that they were trying out on the swamp. "Of course, we'd known since we were little nippers there was *something* there. We used to squeal and carry on, but we never really thought it'd harm us. Eh, Edie?"

"It would've had its work cut out," Edie declared. "We didn't harm easily."

"Did you ever tell anyone?" Simon asked.

"Eh? No fear. You don't go around telling people you've got a Potkoorok in your swamp, do you?"

Simon agreed. He would certainly never have told anyone in the ordinary way. He looked at Charlie, long and lean and wrinkled; and at Edie, bunched in her old rocking chair. He would never have guessed they had ever shared the wonder of Turongs and Potkoorok. "We might be the only white people that ever saw them," he said. The night had turned into a Potkoorok celebration instead of a Nargun horror.

And then there came ringing from the mountains an

ancient, savage cry: *Nga-a-a!* Charlie, Edie, and Simon jerked like puppets. The dogs barked and were silent. The cry died away over the ridges, and Simon managed to fill his lungs again.

"*That's it!*" he whispered staring wide-eyed at the fire. Tiny reflected flames danced in his eyes as if they were made of glass.

"It'll be disappointed then," said Charlie. "It'll get no mutton tonight. We stopped its little game."

"*Doesn't it sound big?*" whispered Simon.

"Noise can't hurt," said Edie. "Do I get any help with the washing up?"

"In a minute," said Charlie. "I was thinking about a fence. How do you think that'd work, Simey? A strong fence, you know, iron posts driven well in and a heavy-gauge chain-wire. We could run a strong fence right around the thing, keep it in one place while we work out what to do about it. What do you think of that?"

Simon tried to uncurl whatever it was that curled up inside him when the Nargun called. "Could you make a fence that strong?" he asked.

Charlie laughed. "Iron posts driven two feet in? It'd take a tank to shift it. What do you think, Edie?"

"It's a start," said Edie. "It might turn out that we don't need it, but it wouldn't hurt to have it there. You'd have to ring up town and see when you could get the stuff for it."

"Do that tomorrow. Simey and I'll have a look tomorrow and see what we need. Eh, Simey?"

"All right," said Simon, feeling a lot better by now. They knew nothing really bad about the Nargun, even from the Potkoorok. There was only the sheep, and Charlie had moved the others. The noise couldn't hurt; maybe they didn't even need the fence, but Charlie would build one anyway. It would be stupid to get worked up.

All the same, when everyone went to bed, Simon left his bedroom door open to the firelight. He was the one who had met the Nargun by moonlight—unless that was a nightmare.

The pine tree whispered against the stars, and the shrill cries of crickets patterned the silence. All the lights were out; only the fire still burned behind its safety screen. The flames made little darting grabs up the chimney, and their light flickered in the windows. Everyone was asleep, even Simon.

The white house settled firm and low on the ridge, its iron roof shining like water in the moonlight. The mountain stood over it, tall and massive, and from there the Nargun looked down. It had dragged itself down its small gully, rocking from limb to limb and grinding moss into the soil, to look at the shoebox house below. It watched for the yellow flicker that sometimes shone from the windows and lit up a shrub or a fence post; and it dreamed of fire.

After a while it moved slowly on, out of the gully. It rocked into stillness and felt beneath it the upward swing of the mountain. It lifted its clumsy head to the moon and felt the silence; the earth and all the shining planets were threaded like beads on that enduring silence.

There had been days that were a moment of irritation to the Nargun; when it had moved restlessly down its small gully to escape from the throbbings and thunders that killed the trees. It was not angry yet, for the moment had been too brief, and as yet it felt no need to leave the mountain. In its cold, heavy way it loved the mountain. It had come to love distance and sky and high rocky places; and though it had killed only a sheep, it knew there were men near. In its cold, still way the Nargun loved men: loved them even when it killed them. Trees that were not yet seeds would be grown and felled and milled before the Nargun chose to leave the mountain.

But in these last days it was restless for a moment, and it sought the peace of night and the star-threaded silence. Now it was soothed; it felt again earth swinging on its moth-flight around the sun. It lowered its head and looked at the shoebox house, watching for the yellow flicker and dreaming of fire. It moved another pace.

Charlie and Simon found it there next day, three yards outside the gully.

7

IT WAS AFTERNOON before Charlie had time to go up the mountain, and Simon went with him. Charlie wanted to see where the fence should go and how long it would need to be to enclose the Nargun; Simon was to hold one end of the measuring string. They were more than half-way to the gully before Charlie slapped his pocket, made a disgusted noise, and confessed that he had left the string behind.

"Sorry, Simey. Have to go back. Wait a bit, though! Where did I leave that rope last time I hauled wood with the tractor? Should be near here." He rode a little way off the track and dismounted. From under one of the logs that he seemed to use as handy toolsheds he dragged out a long coil of rope, which he looked at with satisfaction. "What did I tell you? Always a good idea to keep a thing where it's needed."

They rode on and had almost reached the mouth of the

little high gully before they saw the great stone humped on the ground outside it. They would hardly have believed it could be the same stone if it had not been for that name, SIMON, still showing in the lichen at its base. They stopped in their tracks and stared at it for a moment. Then Charlie dismounted and tethered Surprise to a sapling a little way off, and Simon did the same.

Charlie was silent and frowning. It was one thing to believe, because Simon and Edie did, that a great rock could move up and down the mountain as it wished; it was quite another thing to see it for himself. A small, grim doubt entered his mind that any fence built by humans could hold this bit of ancient earth.

Simon was silent and frowning, too. He had suddenly seen that below the Nargun, a little way down the mountain, lay the house. The white house that closed its walls around you in the dark, and stood steady under the hammers of rain—where firelight flickered on your bedroom door and your mat crept about in the wind and the pine tree whispered outside the window—that was where the Nargun was headed. Simon was so afraid that he was angry instead. He picked up a lump of charred wood and threw it hard at the great crouched stone.

It should have hit—it almost looked as if it had hit—but there was no *thud* of wood on stone or *thunk* of wood on flesh. The wood bounded back hard at Simon, he had to dodge it quickly. And the great hunched stone crouched unmoving, headed toward the house.

The heat of Simon's anger turned cold. He felt frozen,

his eyes fixed on the stone. He didn't hear Charlie speak to him until, after several tries, Charlie clapped him on the shoulder.

"What's up, mate? Ears full of wax?"

Simon whispered, "Charlie—" and gulped. He tried again: "Charlie, watch. Watch, now, keep looking." He groped around for a heavy stick and threw it.

It swung end over end, hard and true toward the big stone and seemed to bounce off some invisible wall and came bounding back. "Duck!" shouted Simon, leaping aside. The stick whizzed by between Charlie and Simon and thudded and bounced on the ground yards behind them.

"M'p," grunted Charlie. "Better be careful what you chuck at that thing, mate." The lines of his face had deepened, and he was lost in thought for a while. At last he spoke in a businesslike way. "I don't reckon we'll wait for the fence, Simey. The way this thing moves about, you must be able to shift it. I reckon we'll give Surprise a try."

Simon's eyes opened wide. "Shift it? Where?"

"Eh?" said Charlie. "Not shift it anywhere, just shift it. Surprise couldn't shift it *away,* it's too much weight for him. We'll just see if he can't rock it a bit or tip it a bit or something."

"Why, Charlie? What good will it do?"

Charlie tried to collect and sort out reasons that he felt rather than saw. "Well. We don't know much about this Nargun thing at all, do we? We don't know if we can fence it, or blast it, or touch it, or what we can do. I reckon we'll have to start finding out, don't you?"

"I—suppose so."

"Well, you just found out something yourself, didn't you? You found you can't chuck something at it without it chucks it back. What if you hadn't found that out? Suppose I'd just lit a fuse and chucked a stick of gelignite. It would've chucked *that* back, just the same as your stick, wouldn't it?"

"I—suppose so."

"And then where would we be? We don't know where we are with this thing at all. We don't even know if we can put a rope around it. Suppose we find out we can, and suppose Surprise gives it a tug and makes it rock or tip up or something, *then* we might try with the truck or the tractor. We might be able to get it on a truck and have it carted off somewhere. I don't think we can just leave it here, do you? And wait and see what happens?"

Simon glanced down at the house and back again. "No," he said quickly. "Only—if it's too heavy for Surprise, wouldn't it be better to try with the tractor straight off?"

"Well, you could have an accident on this slope, with a rock that size. A tractor's got no sense and a horse has. I'd rather have a go with Surprise first."

"All right . . . only, Charlie . . ."

"What's up?"

"Say we did get it on a truck. Where would you cart it off to? Where could you leave it?"

"It's a big country, mate."

"But it might kill someone else's sheep! *It might come back!*"

"Yeah, well, we'll have to think about that. First we have to find out if we can do anything at all. Now you go up there—not inside the gully, up on the edge of it—and keep an eye on that thing while I see what I can do with this rope."

Simon edged a little way up the mountain, full of uneasiness. There was no need to tell him to keep an eye on the Nargun; except for a quick look at Charlie now and then, his eyes could not leave it. It stood humped on the hill, unmoving, on its path to the house. SIMON, it called silently. He could see one dark cavity like an eye half turned to him, as though the darkness knew and watched.

Charlie had laid one end of his rope on the ground ten feet from the Nargun. There was a small loop tied in that end of the rope, and Charlie walked away from it in a wide circle unwinding a trail of rope as he went, making a ring of rope on the ground around the great stone. On the uphill side he stopped for a moment to think, then moved closer in, step by step, to a sapling that grew only a yard or so from the stone. There he laid his trail of rope over a small branch, so that the sapling held the rope a few feet above the ground. Then he went on, finishing his circle and closing the ring of rope. He shook out the rest of the rope and passed his end through the loop that lay on the ground, turning the rope ring into a wide, slack noose. The stone was still, and the dark cavity watched. Simon's knees felt weak. He was sure Surprise could not move the stone, but in the dark places of his mind he dreaded what the stone might do.

Charlie stood with the loose end of rope in his hand and looked about again. Then he called to Simon, "I'll take her round that messmate," pointing to a sturdy tree near him. "She'll pull toward the tree, and Surprise and I will be going the other way. Keep your eyes on that thing —yell if it moves an inch."

Simon nodded. Charlie walked to the tree, flicking the rope delicately so that it slid lightly through the loop. The noose grew a little smaller, but it did not move from the sapling branch. Charlie passed his end of the rope over a shoulder-high branch of the tree and brought Surprise and tied the rope high on a stirrup-leather. Simon saw that the noose, held up by the sapling on one side and the tree on the other, might tighten about the Nargun high up under its blunt muzzle. If that happened, and Surprise were pulling at the top of the rock instead of at its base, then perhaps he might move it a very little. He fixed his eyes on it, ready to shout at the first movement. The great boulder crouched, heavy with stillness, and the dark cavity watched.

The noose drew in; it rose above the ground on all sides; it strained at the sapling branch. Simon could hear Charlie's voice bullying and coaxing Surprise. The sapling sprang and the noose whipped tight—around the neck of the Nargun, under what looked like its head. Simon held his breath: nothing happened. The dark cavity watched.

He glanced away for a moment at Charlie and Surprise. They had rounded the messmate and returned toward the gully. The rope was strained tight: to the tree, around it, and back to Surprise, who was leaning into the leather breastplate of his harness and pulling. Simon looked at the great boulder again. His hands ached from being clenched.

He could not see the dark, vacant eye.

He tried to yell with empty lungs. The rope strained, the rock seemed to rear a little. Simon managed to yell: *"Charlie!"* Then everything happened.

Instantly Charlie steadied Surprise and began to ease him while he looked across to the rock. Slowly, heavily, the great rock moved—not toward the tree with the pull of the straining rope, but like a pendulum, down and across toward man and horse. Surprise fought as Charlie forced him back and away, trying to keep tension on the rope, to use the tree, to untie the knot. Simon kept on yelling.

He could see a rock, heavy and inert, changing course and rolling the wrong way—and he glimpsed rocky limbs levering at the ground, a blunt muzzle snarling, a watchful darkness—

Charlie fought and fumbled—the rock rolled past the horse's heels—he lashed at it and cracked it with a hoof as it passed—a piece broke off and scuttled into the grass uphill—the end of the rope fell loose, and Charlie and Surprise sprang away—the rock lay still.

Simon sat down and put his head on his knees.

In a moment he looked up again. Charlie was still talking to Surprise, and Pet was straining nervously at her
reins. Simon dragged himself up and went to Pet. The
rock lay near with the rope still around it and the loose
end trailing; there was a fresh break near the base where
the piece had chipped off. SIMON, said the rock.

Charlie and Simon looked at their horses and said
nothing. Charlie began to lead Surprise away down the
mountain and Simon followed with Pet. They left the rope
where it was.

"Fool thing to try," said Charlie at last. "Should've set
it up the other way around and used another tree. . . .
Should've used the tractor . . ."

"It wouldn't have made any difference," said Simon
flatly. "Nothing would. It did what it wanted to."

Charlie looked uncomfortable and was silent. After a
moment he said, "I need my head read. Should've known
it'd roll downhill, whichever way the pull went. Only I
never thought Surprise could shift it, not with that rig. It
must've been just balancing."

"It rolled half *across* the hill, not down," said Simon.
"And Surprise had stopped pulling when it started. . . .
Did you see the bit that broke off? It ran away uphill into
the grass."

Charlie gave him a sudden sharp look. "I didn't see
that. And there was too much happening for you to be
sure what you saw. So we won't say anything about it to
Edie, mind." He frowned, pushed his mouse-colored hat
into its worried position, and tugged it down again hard.

"I've got to get the stock back into this paddock soon, and lord knows if that thing'll hold still while I put a fence around it. Maybe I'd better try with the tractor . . ."

Simon broke into a cry: "Don't make it angry, Charlie!" He broke off because it was a useless thing to say, and Charlie couldn't answer it; not until he too had seen the Nargun. So they went on in another uncomfortable silence, leading their upset horses.

When they reached the house, Charlie declared that they were still too busy for a cup. He added cunningly, "We needn't give Edie a look at us till we've settled down a bit. So we'll just get the jobs done first and have a cup after that."

Simon felt sure that nothing would rouse Edie's wonder more than Charlie's failing to appear for his cup; but if Simon knew the Nargun better than Charlie did, Charlie surely knew Edie better than Simon did. He said nothing but helped as usual to feed the animals. It really was late enough. The timber-getters, who had been working today with their chain-saw, though without their bulldozer, had stopped for the day while he and Charlie were coming down the ridge. The hills' great shadows leaned across the ridges, and crickets were shrilling to the silence.

Simon stood watching the cows and horses while they snuffled up their little heaps of chaff from the winter-browned grass. One by one as they finished, they lifted their heads, snorted or blew, and snuffled in the grass again for the last bits of chaff. Simon could wait no longer. Refusing to look at Charlie, who was feeding the dogs and watching, he began to herd the cows and horses down the ridge to the creek. They were as surprised as Charlie, but he didn't let them stop; he shouted and waved his arms and threw bits of stick until they kicked up their heels and ran down the creek to the flat. That was the best he could do.

Coming back, he checked the fowl-run gate. It was well fastened, but the light wire netting of the run looked flimsy and unsafe. Still, hens were very small things, and they roosted quietly in the darkness of their shed. They were probably safe except for accidents. Simon went to the woodheap for an armload of wood, still refusing to look at Charlie.

The sky was cold and pale when they went into the kitchen at last, and smoke from the chimney showed that Edie had already lit the fire. She gave each of them her seeing look and said, "You won't be wanting a cup now it's so late. I'll have dinner on the table by the time you've cleaned up."

"That'll do us," agreed Charlie warmly. "We could eat a horse, eh, Simey? As long as it was Surprise and not old Pet." And he laughed in a way that drew another of Edie's looks. She said nothing more until they were having dinner.

"And how was the Nargun?" she asked then.

"Eh?" said Charlie. Simon kept his eyes on his plate.

"The Nargun. You were going to look at it and see about the fence. Is it still there?"

"That thing," said Charlie, remembering the Nargun

with an effort. "Yes, it's still there. We had a go at shift-ing it with Surprise and a rope, but we only managed to roll it a bit further down the slope."

"Did you measure the fence?"

"Forgot the measuring string," said Charlie. "Have to have another go tomorrow."

Edie looked at Charlie's innocent smile and at Simon examining a baked potato. She retreated into her calmest mood and said nothing more. Charlie made up for this by teasing Simon about old Pet and the Potkoorok and the grader. Dinner had been over for half an hour before Charlie's cheerfulness failed; then, quite suddenly, he grew quiet and strained.

He had heard the dogs give a bark and had gone out-side to listen for foxes. He was away for some time and came back with his face pressed into deeper creases and looking the wrong color. Simon hardly had time to notice, for Edie said, "If you're helping with fencing tomorrow, Simey, you'll need your sleep. I've put your hot-water bag in your bed." And he had to go.

He was sure he wouldn't sleep. In the silence, shrill-edged with crickets, nothing seemed to move. There were no Turong cries; he had heard none since the night they sank the grader. No possum jumped, no bird called, the pine tree was a tall, dark silence. There was nothing to come between him and his memory of the afternoon. He thought of the unmoving stone, darkly watchful; of half-glimpsed shapeless limbs; of the little broken piece that scuttled off uphill. And he found his anger returning.

"You wait, you rotten thing," he whispered. "You just wait." Then, after all, he was able to go to sleep.

He slept heavily, for he had been through days and nights of strain; yet twice in the night he half woke. Once it was to find Charlie in the room shutting the window. Half asleep, Simon thought there must be another storm. The second time he woke because his door was open and the room quite light. He got up and went stumbling to shut the door, feeling that it was very late and the light should not still be on. It was not. From his door he could see the fire, still fresh, filling the room with strong yellow light—and Charlie stretched out in his old chair beside it, dozing. Simon shut his sleepy eyes on the scene and went back to bed.

Simon slept on: and Charlie stayed in his chair all night. He dozed a little sometimes and woke to feed the fire and listen, to walk softly through the house and listen again. Once he went to his study and riffled through drawers until he found an old cigar box. He took it back to the living room and put it on the mantelpiece. Two or three times Edie crept softly in her dressing gown and with tousled hair to look at him. Her face was still and her eyes serious in the firelight. Each time she stole away again without being seen and went back to lie in her own bed and listen too.

Charlie and Edie heard nothing. Peering through dark windows into darkness, they saw nothing. Only once, strained wires creaked when something heavy leaned against the gate; once the firelight, spilling through the window, threw a great crooked shadow on Edie's roses. And once, when Edie looked out at the dark, she was caught in a huge, lost loneliness as though the dark looked back. An ancient hunger, a fumbling, formless love, held her for a moment at the window. Then it passed, and Edie crawled shivering back to bed and lay awake.

That hungering darkness drained away at last. The night was alive again with the secret life of possum and mopoke and fox. The Turongs called. Charlie rose stiffly and went to bed for three or four hours. Everyone in the white house slept at last while the Nargun drew slowly away, foot by foot up the ridge, trailing Charlie's rope. Charlie went to look for it at first light and found it back inside its small gully. It had seen the fire.

The rope had slipped off by then and lay caught on a rock, flattened and frayed in one place where something hard and heavy had ground it. Charlie looked at it for some time before he picked it up and coiled it neatly. He took it back to the shed and went in for breakfast.

Simon was sitting in his place at the table, and Edie was frying sausages. She looked at Charlie as he came in, and he stopped in the doorway and looked back. There was a kind of shock on both their faces. Then Charlie went to the sink to wash his hands, and Edie began to dish up fried tomato.

Neither of them spoke, and Simon was silent too; but

he knew that in the night something had changed. He felt afraid and comforted, both at the same time; and he felt strong enough to help in any way that was needed.

Charlie and Edie would know what to do now. They had seen the Nargun.

8

"I DON'T KNOW about that fence," Charlie confessed. "I reckon we need help. We don't know enough about this thing."

"We'd have our work cut out," Edie pointed out. "We never even saw one before, and it's not our kind. How could we know?"

"I know, mate. That's why I reckon we'll have to talk to the old things. They ought to be able to tell us something about it; we're just guessing as it is. They might even help."

"They won't want to," Simon warned. "The Potkoorok said they don't go near. They don't even want to talk about it—I don't think it's *their* kind, either."

"M'p," said Charlie. "But they've known me a bit longer than they've known you. You don't even know the drill for it yet, you've just been lucky. And I've got a thing or two to say that could change their minds for them. We'll go as quick as we can. I've got the horses ready. What about you, Edie? Want to come?"

"You might be needing me later," said Edie. "I'll keep things going here while I can."

"Simey could give you a hand, only I might need him. I haven't talked to the old things since we were kids."

"Have you still got the stick?"

"Rustled it out last night. It's on the mantelpiece." He went inside and came back with a cigar box, which he opened. Simon glimpsed a length of plaited leather, a gold tiepin with a horseshoe on it, a flashlight shaped like a revolver, and other old treasures. Charlie took out a stick about six inches long with one end carved in crisscross lines that made a pattern of diamonds. He buttoned it into his shirt pocket and put the box on top of the refrigerator. "Ready, young feller? The old things like it early or late, they're not much for the middle of the day."

Edie came with them to the gate. "Where is that thing, then?" she called after them.

"Back in the gully—no need to worry," called Charlie, giving Simon a quick leg up onto Pet. Then they were on their way, waving to Edie as they went.

"What's the stick?" asked Simon.

"Our old message-stick," said Charlie. "You'll have to be getting one for yourself."

"Why? What's it for?"

"Well, in this country, when you want to talk to someone, you don't go barging into his territory yelling for him like you did. You send a messenger with a message-stick, or take it yourself if you're stuck, and then sit down and wait till he decides to take notice. That's manners."

"Who told you that?"

"The old Potkoorok. It smartened up Edie's and my manners quick, and I'm surprised it hasn't started on yours by now. But you'll see how it's done today when you take my stick for me. Then you can carve one of your own, and every time they see it after that, they'll know you're visiting."

"Wouldn't they know if I just sat down and waited without the stick?"

"Why should they? You might be just sitting there not thinking about them, or you might be starting in to chop down their trees. The message-stick is a promise that you're coming in a friendly way."

"And if I wasn't, they could play their tricks on me. . . ."

"That's about the size of it. If you want a friendly talk, you take your message-stick and mind your manners."

"All right," said Simon. "There's the chain-saw starting up. I wonder how long they'll keep going without a bull-dozer?"

"Not long. There's not enough milling timber in that old scrub, it's been through too many fires. The clearing's the main job, and they need a 'dozer for that. Bad luck losing one when they were nearly through."

"Nearly through?"

"Well, they were leaving timber for shade and camps, and they'd cleared a good area. They reckoned they only had two or three days' work left."

Charlie spoke absently and then fell into a silence. They were within sight of the swamp, and Simon wondered if the Turongs and the Potkoorok would talk to a grown-up man; and how Charlie would feel, seeing them again after all these years. It would feel better than seeing the Nargun, anyway. Perhaps Charlie was thinking and frowning about that. The scream of the chain-saw was caught in a trap of silence, but the little cries of the frogs went free. Torn scraps of mist littered the hills and were slowly sucked up, as if the sun were drinking them through a straw.

"Now then," said Charlie, swinging down from Surprise and waiting for Simon to scramble off Pet, "you take this stick and go down to the bank at the far end. Sit down with your back to the water—that's important—and hold the stick up plain, and just wait. You might have to wait some time, or the old Potkoorok mightn't come at all. If it does, you stand up. Then you say: 'Charlie Waters sent me. He used to be a boy on this place, and now he's the man in charge. He wants to talk to you.' "

"But you're not the man in charge! You own it!"

"Do I? For sixty years or so, maybe; but how long do you think the Potkoorok's owned it?"

"M'p . . ." said Simon. "All right. Then what do I do?"

"You come back and tell me what it says. I'll hitch the horses somewhere and wait here."

"I always use a branch of that log. Will it take two?"

"Just the ticket," said Charlie, with his serious inward smile. "Off you go."

Simon went, carrying the gray old stick carefully. He sat as Charlie had said, holding the stick with its carved end up like a candle. It was a long minute before the green-gold Potkoorok came over the bank from behind him. Its wide mouth was turned down with self-importance, and Simon stood up at once. He felt irritated, all the same. He would rather bribe it with apples and sit beside it in a friendly way than go through all this fuss.

The Potkoorok spoke with sober politeness. "The Frog Boy comes from the Boat Boy. I thought that boy was gone."

"He's a man now," said Simon and the Potkoorok looked huffy. "He's in charge of all this place," boasted Simon, and it gave a snort. "He wants to talk to you," finished Simon.

The Potkoorok stood silent for a moment while the frogs sang to the sun. At last it said, "Bring the Man in good will," and sat down on the bank.

Simon went back to Charlie. "I can bring you in good will, but I don't think it's keen. You ought to try an apple next time."

"None of your lip," said Charlie. "You're just the messenger around here, and mind you don't interrupt."

They went back to where the Potkoorok was sitting, and Charlie sat down beside it draping his long legs over the bank and pushing his mouse-colored hat into the forward position. "Been a long time," he said.

The Potkoorok chuckled wickedly. "Long for you, Boat Boy. A day for me."

"A long time for old friends," said Charlie firmly. "I've left this place alone, haven't I? Even in dry times when I could use the water. I've never cut a tree without I had to, even though the place is too small, really, and I could use the grass. That's because we're old friends, me and you and the Turongs."

The Potkoorok looked sideways from its golden eyes and was silent. Charlie pulled a stem of grass and chewed it, staring at the swamp.

"I remember my old grandfather building this bank," he said. "It didn't work, he couldn't afford to make it long enough. Easy now, with the machinery we've got—you could clear that bit of scrub in a week with a bulldozer, like they've been doing on the far ridge. But a man doesn't want to lose old friends, I say."

"And what does the old friend want of the Potkoorok?" asked the creature sulkily.

"Eh?" said Charlie. "Oh, that. Well, just a bit of advice, and maybe a bit of help. But I wanted to talk to you and the Turongs together. If I sent my boy up to ask them, would they come down here, do you think?"

"Why should they?" said the Potkoorok grandly. "They will not remember the Boat Boy or know the Man in Charge. Can Turongs dive into water when strangers come? They dive into trees—not so good as water—they cannot help it. They are Turongs, creatures of the trees."

"Bad luck," said Charlie. "What can we do, then?"

"The Boy will take *my* message to the Turongs, for the Potkoorok can dive into trees as well as water. And the Potkoorok is an old friend known to the Turongs. If they welcome us, then we will talk in the forest." It slid down under the water.

"You were threatening!" said Simon, shocked. "You were saying you'd drain the swamp and cut down the scrub if they didn't help!"

"You want to get something done about those ears, mate," said Charlie. "I said I wouldn't want to lose old friends, and that's a fact. The old Pot-K knows what's what. Nobody could drain this swamp—how do you think they managed to hide the grader in it? And a bulldozer couldn't work on that slope. Trouble is, the old thing's huffy because I've grown up on it. I had to give it some excuse for helping a grown man."

The Potkoorok rose with water running down its green skin and something clutched in its fingers. Simon saw that its message-stick was a stone engraved with fossil shells. He stood up, and the Potkoorok gave him the stone.

"You will go among the first trees," it said, "and sit with your eyes on the swamp. When the Turongs come you will speak so." It threw back its head as if it were addressing a meeting. " 'The Potkoorok greets the Turongs. The Potkoorok would bring the Man in Charge to talk with them. He will not kill the forest if the Turongs are his friends."

"Charlie didn't say—" began Simon hotly.

"Thought I told you not to interrupt," said Charlie.

"Go," said the Potkoorok. "We cannot tell what the Man thinks. We know only what he says."

"You *don't*," said Simon. "You know what he does, too. He's a good friend, and if he wants help you ought to give it to him. That's if *you're* a good friend."

"*Simey*, what did I tell you?"

"What is good?" said the Potkoorok. "What is friend? The mountain is my friend, and the stars. They do not vanish when I close my eyes and leave me lonely."

"Good for you, then," said Simon. "I hope they help you when you want it, and plant new trees, and—all *right*, I'm going."

"And mind you say just what you were told to say," Charlie called after him.

Simon strode angrily up to the scrub. Just inside the first trees he sat on a root terrace holding up the Potkoorok's message-stick and frowning down at the swamp. Charlie and the Potkoorok were sitting peacefully on the bank looking up toward him. Perhaps they really were still friends.

He heard nothing but the stirring of leaves. He saw nothing till the thin gray shadows with their floating beards came sliding and circling down the trunks beside him. There were four of them, holding out spidery fingers for the message-stick. He stood up and gave it to one of them, repeating the Potkoorok's message as well as he could. Seeing them close and by daylight, he suddenly thought the message might be wise even if it wasn't fair. It might need a threat or bribe to hold these wispy, elusive creatures.

The Turongs retired to talk about the message—in two steps they had vanished. Simon could hear their rustling whispers quite near; and after a moment they were there again holding out the message-stick.

"Bring the Potkoorok and the Man in peace," they said.

Simon took the stone and went out through the trees. He waved to Charlie and shouted, "Hoi! You can come!" Charlie's skinny length rose from the bank and came striding up, with the Potkoorok leaping and bobbing beside it. Simon took the chance to have a close look at the spirals of fossil shells on the stone he was holding—until flattened green fingers whisked it out of his hands.

"Oh—hallo," he said. "I can bring you in peace." And he led the way into the scrub.

A great crowd of Turongs had collected. Shadowy shapes stood among dead leaves—clustered on low branches—came and went from the treetops and scuttled like spiders around trunks. There was a constant hissing and rustling of whispers. Wherever you looked, straggling beards were clustered and sly dark eyes looked away. They made Simon feel shy, but Charlie only nodded and waited. The Potkoorok waited too; it seemed to be manners that the people of the place should speak first.

At last one of them did speak in a voice like leaves. "The water-spirit is here."

The Potkoorok replied in its own gurgling voice, pointing to Charlie. "The Man in Charge is here too. You knew him when he was the Boat Boy. He comes for help. Let him be our friend for the sake of our water and trees. Talk, Boat Boy."

"Glad to see you again," said Charlie. "It's this stone thing on the mountain, this Nargun."

The hissing and rustling stopped, and the scuttling of feet in dead leaves. The movement in treetops and branches was still. Hundreds of eyes glanced sideways and away. Everything was quiet.

Charlie went on calmly. "This Nargun's not a friendly thing like the rest of us. It wanders around the place at night, and it's killed a sheep already. It's big enough to be dangerous, and I don't think we can do with it here. I'd like to get rid of it."

The Potkoorok's face was comical and sober. It said, "We do not know the Nargun. It is a stranger. We do not help you, Boat Boy."

"Well, that's just it," said Charlie, as if he and the Potkoorok had reached an agreement at last. "It's a stranger here. It doesn't belong on Wongadilla, and I reckon it should go."

"It should go," the Potkoorok agreed.

"So I thought at least you'd be able to tell me something about it. If I knew a bit about it I might be able to get rid of the thing."

The Potkoorok spoke to the Turongs. "What can we tell the Boat Boy of the Nargun?"

Their silence was broken by rustlings and hissings. After a while the voices rose like wind in the trees until they began to chant in a wind corroboree: "The Nargun should go! Back to its country! Back to the south land!" "Leave our land, Nargun! Leave Wongadilla! This land is our land!" Those in the trees were swaying as they chanted; those on the ground were stamping and shuffling. "Back to its old den! Back to the south land! The Nargun must go!"

This might have gone on as long as the wind, but the Potkoorok broke in with a corroboree of its own, jumping up and down and booming, "Hear the Boat Boy! Let him talk! Hear the Boat Boy! Let him talk!" until the Turongs began to listen and fall silent. At last they were all quiet again, watching with their sly dark eyes.

"That's good then," said Charlie. "If that's how you feel, you won't mind helping." There was an uneasy stirring. Even the Potkoorok was uneasy. "I don't know what to do with this thing. If you throw something at it, what you throw comes back. If you pull on it with a rope it comes straight for you. If you break a bit off—well, I don't know, but the boy says the bit runs away."

"What breaks off the Nargun is a Nargun," the Potkoorok explained in a low voice.

"There you are then. You know more about it than I do. Its your sort, not mine. You ought to be able to tell me." Silence. "I thought about fire," Charlie coaxed. "If I set a fire in the top gully, would that drive it away?"

"Not fire," said the Potkoorok. "Fire is its dreaming."

"Take a bulldozer to it and bury it, then?"

"Bury it? Earth is its self and its being."

"Well, there must be something. How did the tribes manage? What did they do?"

"They listened to its cry and stayed by the campfires. They walked wide of its den or were lost. We can do nothing, Boat Boy."

"Well, that's a nice thing," said Charlie sternly. "There's a lot of you Turongs, a minute ago all shouting war cries. Can't any of you *tell* me anything?"

The Turongs stirred again. There were whispers, growing louder, until at last a few voices could be heard: "The Nyols!" "Ask the Nyols!" "They know the rocks and the places in the earth." "Ask the Nyols."

The Potkoorok opened its old eyes wider. "The Nyols," it said, considering.

"Never heard of 'em," said Charlie.

"You hear now . . . they do live in caves and know stone."

"Where do I find them?"

"Where the mountain ends. There is rock above the forest. The Nyols live in the rock."

"I don't know any caves there," said Charlie.

The Potkoorok looked at him slyly. "The Man in Charge finds the caves when he finds the Nyols. Let the Boy take your message. At the back of the mountain he will find them."

"I'll let you know, then. I suppose I can say we come from the Turongs?"

They nodded, and their beards rose and fell.

"Well, if that's the best you can do, thanks. Come on, Simey." Charlie turned and strode down the hill with Simon following. The Potkoorok came bobbing and leaping after them a moment later and caught up.

"Not much thanks," it said reproachfully.

"Not much help," said Charlie. "I don't go much on this Nyols idea. I reckon you old things are putting me off."

"Never call us old when the Nargun comes," said the Potkoorok. It spoke softly—but inside Simon something curled up again like a leaf in the flame. "How old am I, Boat Boy?"

Charlie gave it a sudden look. "How would I know, old-timer? I might guess, I suppose. As old as the water you live in?"

It turned its clumsy head away and chuckled. "Not so wrong, maybe. In this form or that. And the Turongs?"

"That's trickier. As old as the leaves? Or a lizard's skin?"

It chuckled again. Then it said soberly, "And what was before the water, Boat Boy? What was before the lizard and the leaves?" Charlie was silent. After a moment the old creature went on. "The Man in Charge can drain the water, cut down the trees, bang the lizard with a stick. But what will he do with the rock? What will he do with the ground he stands on and the forces and fires that live in it? What will you do with the Nargun, Man?"

Simon shuddered. They reached the swamp before

Charlie answered. Then he stood by his horse and looked grimly at the Potkoorok. "Hard to say, old-timer," he said. "As to the ground I stand on, I reckon I'll live on it for the time I've got and do the best I can with it. And after me some other man. As to the rest, I'll have to take another look, that's all. Right, Simey? Or do you want a leg up?"

9

CHARLIE AND SIMON rode home deep in silence. Charlie's face was lined with thought. He had learned only that the Nargun was something dark and ancient from the earth, and that he had already learned last night; but he had to think about it. Simon's thoughts circled around the unknown Nyols, living in rocks and earth. He was telling himself that they couldn't be very different from these others, or surely the Potkoorok would not have said that Simon should go and find them . . . but if he did go he would have to put the Nargun between himself and Charlie and Edie. He would be alone with these Nyols, whatever they were, with the Nargun between him and home.

Edie saw them from the fowl-run as they came down the ridge. She waved a hand that was holding two eggs and hurried into the kitchen. Charlie said, "We'll want the horses," so they hitched them at the shed and went inside. Edie was already pouring tea.

"No good?" she said, looking at their faces.

"Not much," said Charlie. "We found out a bit, most of it bad, and they won't help."

"It might've been asking a bit much," she suggested. "They mightn't want to help against their own kind."

"I don't think that comes into it," said Charlie. "This Nargun's come into their territory where it's got no right. They want to see it go, but it's got them bluffed."

"I think they ought to help," said Simon crossly.

Edie smiled a little. "Poor old things. They can't be more than they are. They just play tricks, that's all. When the bush was full of people hunting and fishing to live, they and their tricks must have been quite important. It must be an empty life for them now, but still they can't turn into something different. I shouldn't think this Nargun's going to be fooled by a few tricks."

"You never know," said Charlie. "That's the trouble. But they might've tried already, of course." He gave Edie a proper account of the meeting. She looked astonished to hear of the Nyols but stayed quiet till the end. Then she sat quiet a while longer.

"If it's rock and fire and—the earth—" began Simon. Charlie interrupted.

"You heard it wrong. The Potkoorok's not water, you know. It just—belongs to water. It meant the same as that about the Nargun."

"Still—maybe it's not all bad. . . ."

"Nothing's all bad," said Edie.

116

"Makes no difference," added Charlie. "That's pretty powerful stuff, what the old Potkoorok was trying to say. I'm not having a power like that loose on my land, killing sheep and frightening people and lord knows what. It can go back where it belongs. We can't live with it."

"Not right beside us," Edie agreed. "A power like that has to be a good way off."

"But Charlie, *maybe there's nothing we can do?*"

"There's something," said Charlie. "We've just got to find out what. Look, Simey—if a power like that had nothing to stop it, where would it be after all these ages? King of the world, everyone bowing down to it. But even the tribes didn't bow down to this Nargun, from what the old things said. And the tribes lived with it. No, we've just got to find out how to handle it."

"I suppose these Nyols *might* help," said Edie. "Can you go yourself? Or me?"

"The old Pot-K said send the boy, so I reckon they won't show for us."

"Well, Simey can't go. We don't know what they're like."

"Not much help if he did go, probably. No, I reckon the best we can do is hang around up there and keep a close watch on that stone thing and see what we can see."

"I *can* go," said Simon. He could feel two pairs of gray eyes exploring his face like fingers. "I've got to go—it's the only thing the others told us. The Potkoorok wouldn't say to go if the Nyols were dangerous."

"They don't know the message-stick," said Edie to Charlie. "They wouldn't take any notice of it, would they?"

"They might," said Charlie. "Word gets around. But I can't let Simey go back behind the mountain by himself on the chance, and I won't waste my own time going on the chance. I want to keep an eye on this Nargun."

"You'll be up there, then," Simon pointed out. "You'll be close. I'll go up with you and hop on over the hill. It's not far. You'll know if I don't come straight back, and you can come and look for me."

"And a fat lot of good it might be by then."

But Simon found himself arguing hotly. "Look, I've got to go, there isn't anything else. I mean I know you're going to watch, and I s'pose you'll find out best what to do, and then maybe you won't want to do that either. I mean we went to the *swamp* to find out, and we found out about the *Nyols,* and now you don't want to *do* it. We *have* to do things, don't we?"

"You don't," said Charlie. "Edie and I have to do what we can, no question. It's our land, and we have to look out for it—"

"You said it was mine!" shouted Simon, red in the face. "Some day if I wanted it, you said! I found that Nargun, and it's got my name on it! What am I supposed to do, then? Go and live in a Home for about fifty years and then come and say all-right-I-want-it-now? What do you want me here for if I'm not supposed to do the same as you?"

"Look here—" Charlie was beginning warmly, when Edie cut in.

"What's all this fuss about? If you're going, Simey, you'd better get out there on Pet and stop holding Charlie up before he loses his patience with you. And don't go rushing off without your lunch, you'll need it." She put wrapped packages into their hands and herded them out of the kitchen. "Don't worry about getting back, I can manage." She watched from the gate as they mounted. "Don't get too close to that thing, Charlie!" she called, waving them off. "You take care, now, Simey, and mind what Charlie tells you!"

They started up the ridge in awkward silence. Simon was most astonished by his own sudden fury and embarrassed about the things he had said. He looked for a way to break the silence until he noticed a certain quality in it and looked suspiciously at Charlie. Sure enough, Charlie's face was wooden: the silence was quivering with his inward laughter.

"What's it like at the back of the mountain?" said Simon.

"Haven't seen it much," said Charlie. "No need to. Pretty rocky, though. I'm not real keen on you climbing around it on your own, and that's a fact. You don't know the place yet. And there's no sense anyone climbing around rocks on his own; you always need two for safety."

Simon didn't want to start all that again. He said, "Where will you be, then?"

119

"Just inside the top gully, as far as I know. Sticking to that stone thing like a tick. And as soon as you get back you can take a turn yourself."

"Only it doesn't move in daylight. We mightn't see anything for weeks."

"We'll see that it never moves in daylight, then—unless you pull on it with a rope, anyhow. We'll see if birds light on it, and if it ever scratches, and if it gets wet in the rain. We'll watch it till dark, and maybe see when it does start to move. If we can't frighten it off with fire, we'll see if we can coax it. In the end we'll find out something."

"But we won't make it angry . . . and we won't get anyone to help. . . . Why not, Charlie?"

"Not their job," Charlie suggested. "More likely, they'd think we were mad, and someone'd get killed trying to prove it."

"*We* won't get killed, though."

"Not us. We won't take our eyes off it and we won't touch it. We'll just find out how to send it where it belongs."

"*I* touched it . . . I wish it didn't still have my name on it."

"Never you mind about that, mate. It's the one'll be sorry for that in the end. When it gets to wherever it's going, it can thank your name for sending it there."

"The poor thing!" cried Simon, suddenly full of pity.

Charlie threw him a look. "It's only got to go back where it came from. Or some harmless place. That's all."

They had ridden on past the gully mouth and up the

zigzag track. The chain-saw howled from below. All the mist had gone, leaving the morning warm and bright. Charlie pointed out the way around the mountain.

"You can see, at the base of the high rocks, the ground bulges out a bit before it drops to the ridge. If you follow that bulge it'll take you around the back safe enough, and if you don't find the Nyols by then, just come straight home. Still got the old stick?"

"In my pocket," said Simon.

"Right. You know the drill now. Just see what they've got to say. Shove your lunch into your pockets, you might need it. Will you leave Pet up here, or do you want me to lead her down?"

Simon hesitated. "I'll ride her down. And I'll find you in the Nargun's gully, won't I?"

"Unless I find you first. I don't reckon you can get lost on the mountain, but if you do, remember to stay put."

"Lost!" said Simon indignantly. It seemed rather late to start worrying about that.

At Charlie's new stretch of fence, he dismounted and hitched Pet in the shade. He made his lunch into separate packets and pushed them into different pockets.

"You don't have to go, you know," said Charlie. "I could do with a hand watching this stone thing. I'd sooner, really. You'd better come on back."

"They said to go," said Simon, almost apologizing. "See you, Charlie." He started up the mountain. When he looked back, Charlie was riding away down the track.

Now that he was by himself, he stood still for a moment. He felt lost already, with the Nargun below him and the unknown Nyols somewhere in front. His hands were suddenly sticky, and he wiped them on his jeans. If he went back down the mountain after Charlie and said, "I'm not going," Charlie would say, "Good, I could do with a hand," and it would be all right. He sat down with his back against a tree.

"It's because everything's happened so fast," he decided. Five days since they sank the grader and a shadow loomed at him in the dark. Three days since he came up here to be alone and found the stone, with his name on it, missing. In those three days he had never been alone except in bed. He was glad of Charlie and Edie now, but still he needed some time alone. And everything had happened so fast.

Now, after three days, he was back on the mountain above Wongadilla, and he was alone. There were the plunging green depths, the slopes the color of moonlight and of hay; there were the heights swinging up beyond, shadowed with blue and purple. And here, beneath him, was the strength of the mountain. All about lay the spinning world with the dark forests riding it and strands of creek and river clinging to it and birds netted in its clear, cold air. This patch was Wongadilla, and it was his too; and it was beautiful.

He stood up again and spoke, not shouting in case Charlie heard: "I'm Simon Brent, if anyone wants to know. And where my name is, I put it there." He waited, but no stones cried out. The spinning world kept to its thrum of silence, and Simon set off to find the Nyols.

In coming down from Pet and walking this little way he had lost sight of the shelf of ground around the end of the mountain. He had passed the place where he should have climbed under Charlie's fence and decided it wasn't worth going back. He had climbed to the top of the mountain before, and if he went over the top, he must come to the other side. So he climbed again above the tangled ridges, turned his back to Wongadilla, and started down the slope.

At first it was steep but not difficult. Then, all at once, he was on the edge of a cliff. He tucked his arm around a tree and looked over.

The cliff was only about fifteen feet high, with an easy slope of grass and stones below: that must be this end of Charlie's bulge, that he should have followed. It would be a nuisance to go all the way back to its beginning and follow it around; he must be able to climb down this little rock face.

He thought he probably could: there were crags and little waterways. He decided to try for as long as the going was easy and to climb back if it grew tricky. Then he would just have to go back to Charlie's bulge and take the easy, long way. He found a place where water probably rushed down in storms, and lowered himself into it.

It wasn't as easy as it looked. The footholds were often narrow cracks that his feet slid into sideways; the crags that he clung to were often so wide that he couldn't lower himself far enough. But he thought he could still get back if he had to and kept on—until an edge that looked safe broke away in his hands. He was perched on a sloping surface without a hold to pull himself back. He was stuck.

He kept still, leaning against the cliff and wondering what to do. He must be at least halfway down; perhaps he could jump. But he would need to spring clear of jutting rocks, and he was much more likely to fall. While he perched there thinking about it, he thought he heard a whispering in the rocks.

"Don't be mad," he told himself. "There's enough trouble without going crackers." He eased one foot gently in its crack.

But the whispers went on, with sometimes a soft rumble of laughter. Little dry hands clutched at his ankles, his wrists, his hair. He kicked at them as much as he could without falling. They began to tug, quite strongly, and the chuckles rumbled again. Simon was pulled and tugged into some invisible opening in the rock. There was darkness like a bandage about his eyes.

"Hey!" he shouted. "What's going on?"

The chuckles rumbled in front and behind, echoes falling away and coming back in the dark. Now he could see a little: a shadowy space, a crowd of shadowy forms, and everywhere the crystal gleam of eyes.

"Hey!" shouted Simon, and the echoes came back from far and farther: *hey-ey-ey-hey-hey!* "Are you Nyols?" *Ol-ny-ny-ol-ols?* "Because if you are, I'm looking for you!"

The soft chuckles rumbled back and forth. "You look

for us, we catch you!" called soft, happy voices. Their echoes died away, and they spoke again. "You wrestle," they said.

"Eh?" said Simon. He could see vistas of darkness reaching away amid rock and up and down. There were columns and flowing shapes, dusty but gleaming with lime crystals; he had no idea where the light came from to show them. He could hear a silver gong of water dripping into a pool.

"You wrestle," said the eager voices again. "Now."

"Rot," said Simon. "There's no time. I've got a message." He fumbled in his pocket and held up Charlie's message-stick, like a candle in the gloom.

The Nyols flowed around him in a tide of small gray bodies, fixing bright, curious eyes on the stick.

"It's from Charlie Waters. He's the Man in Charge," boasted Simon, "and he could blow this place wide open with dynamite if he wanted to. Only he doesn't, because he's a good sort. He sent me because the Turongs said to."

Whispers swirled around the cavern and ebbed away beyond. The tide of bodies swept closer; small hands seized Simon and tugged. "You come," they said, and drew him deeper into the heart of the mountain. Simon thought that now they were treating him as a messenger and not as a catch—but they were so strong that he thought they could have dragged him in any case.

He hoped they would not suddenly leave him, for no one could ever find his way out of this cavern. It twisted and curved, rose and fell, with winding ways leading up and down. Its floor was heaved into humps and hills of stone, among which the Nyols hurried him on. He wondered if the faint light came from their eyes. Sometimes there were echoes; sometimes the cavern widened and sounds ran away and were lost. Stalactites as thick as tree trunks made brittle pillars under broad shelves of stone or flowed in salt-cascades over slopes of stone. All of them were covered in powdery dust and half seen in shadows. The Nyols led him down into deeper levels and stopped at last on a broader, flatter floor. All at once the crowd swirled away, leaving Simon alone in an open space while they sat or squatted on rocks along one side.

"Speak," they said.

This must be their meeting place, and they were waiting for his message. Simon paused to gather his wits, listening to the whispers and the dry shuffle of small feet in the dust. Rows of eyes gleamed in dark faces, and over them spread a canopy of rock. That would be a higher floor if you found the slope of rock that led up to it. . . . There was something there, on the wide stone shelf above the Nyols' heads. He could see a yellow shape in the shadow.

"Hey!" cried Simon, speaking at last. "That's the bulldozer! How did it get in here?"

Its proud yellow dim in the shadows, but blunt and powerful as ever like a beast in a cage, the bulldozer was imprisoned in the mountain.

10

SIMON STARED at the bulldozer. "It was you that pinched it!" he cried.

The Nyols grinned at each other with shy pride and kept an uneasy watch on Simon.

He was looking now at the shelf of rock where the bulldozer stood, following along it with his eyes to find the way down. He traced the falling level to a point behind him, opposite the Nyols on their perches, and hurried over there. The voices of the Nyols rumbled like stones. Simon had only put a foot on the upward path before the crowd was around him.

"Ours!" they said. "You come back. You have message—speak."

"Hang on," Simon objected. "I only want to have a look—"

It was useless; he had no chance at all. The small gray bodies bore him back with no effort.

"I wasn't going to touch it," he said huffily. "It's not mine. You can do what you like with it for all *I* care."

They smiled at him. "You speak. We hear," they said kindly, going back to their seats like a well-behaved audience.

"All right," said Simon. He began to tell them about the Nargun.

It was hard to keep his mind on it, with the bulldozer just in front of him. Simon began to play a sort of game as he talked. He never lifted his eyes to the high shelf above but turned his head from side to side and began to step back a little now and then, as if he found it hard to keep his audience in focus. He was sure that they would stop him and make him return, but they seemed to be simple creatures and to take no notice. "Can't see you all, there's so many," he said once; and they chuckled at his difficulty and let him move another two steps back. At last he stood on a hump of stone only two yards from where the upward slope began, and there he stayed and talked in earnest. He had won his game and got home on the Nyols; there was no other idea in his mind just then.

The Nyols nodded their heads solemnly to all he said. They seemed to understand and to agree with the other old things that the Nargun should go away.

"Well, *we* can't make it go," said Simon. "The Turongs thought you might know more about it because of living in stone all the time."

They smiled importantly and nodded again.

"So you'll help us, then?" he asked.

They all shook their heads.

"Well why *not*, for heaven's sake? You just *said* it should go."

There was a soft chorus of agreement. "The Nargun should go," they all said.

"And you just said you knew about it." They smiled and nodded. "Well, you could tell us something about it, couldn't you?"

They all shook their heads again.

"That's mad," said Simon crossly. "*Why* can't you help?"

They told him, in their chorus of soft rumbling voices. "Stone is our dreaming." "That Nargun, that strong stone." "Clever stone."

"Oh . . ." said Simon. "But you could just *tell* us about it, couldn't you? That wouldn't be helping. We only want it to go to its own place."

"We not tell," they said, and began to mutter to each other in a hundred voices. Listening, he picked out some of what they said: "We help Nargun." "Man not move Nargun." "Man not thunder to shake the mountain."

"Oh . . ." said Simon again. Yet he thought they had told him more than they meant to tell. He said, "Thunder drives the Nargun away, doesn't it?"

They only shook their heads again and said, "We not help."

"Bad luck," said Simon. "Have a sandwich, anyway."

He took Edie's lunch out of his pocket and tossed the packages across the cavern to the feet of the Nyols. They scrambled down to poke curiously at these gifts and to tear at the wrappings; and Simon turned and ran quickly and softly up the sloping ledge to the bulldozer.

It couldn't have got where it was by coming this way—not even with the powerful little gray bodies pushing it. The ledge was not a wide enough ramp, and sometimes it was blocked by pillars of rock that Simon had to work around. But it took him along and up two sides of the cavern to the shelf where the bulldozer stood. As he ran the last few yards, he could look down at the Nyols directly below.

They were clustered thickly around the scattering of sandwiches, biscuits, and apples. Those in the front rank were breaking off small pieces of bread or biscuit, sniffing at them doubtfully or putting morsels in their mouths and spitting them out, passing broken crusts to the crowd behind. One of them rolled an apple over the rock, and three or four of them chased it with chuckles. Simon did not think his lunch would hold their attention much longer. But he scrambled into the bulldozer hoping that the darkness under its canopy might hide him a moment longer. He only wanted to sit there for a minute and prove that it was real.

It seemed to be quite normal and unharmed, the great yellow monster shadowed deep inside the mountain. The only damage he could see was to its chimneylike exhaust;

that had broken off short, taking the muffler with it and leaving jagged, rust-flaked edges to show why it had broken. Simon touched levers very lightly and imagined it springing to life beneath him.

It was darker up here, and he could feel the bulging rock of the roof looming close. Then, from behind the bulldozer, he felt a breath of air. Was there an empty blackness there? Had he found a passage to the outside of the mountain? He thought there must be one, or how could the bulldozer have come here?

That was all he had time to notice. The Nyols had lost interest in his lunch and remembered Simon himself. Their bright eyes found him at once, and with rumbles of alarm they came in waves. One stream came along the ramp as Simon had done; the rest swarmed up pillars of rock and dusty crystal and sprang from each other's shoulders to catch the edge of the shelf. Their dry, soft bodies rustled like bats as they swept over the bulldozer. Simon was lifted out like a toy. Crying, "Hang on! I didn't hurt it—I only wanted—" he was passed from hand to hand and lowered to other small hands below till he was standing again amid the ruins of his lunch "—to *look* at it!" finished Simon indignantly.

The Nyols ringed him around. "You wrestle," they said, stern and unsmiling.

"I can't wrestle! Anyhow, I bet no one could wrestle with you little monsters." He began to be afraid from the way they looked that they would keep him there until he did wrestle. He fumbled in his pocket again for Charlie's message-stick and held it up. "I'm a messenger. You have to treat me right."

"You speak," they said, but they did not go back to their seats on the rocks.

"I did speak. I told you about the Nargun, and you said you wouldn't help."

"We not help. You go."

"All right. But I'm going that way. Through that hole." He pointed up toward the bulldozer.

"We take you that way," they said.

They closed around and bore him away: pushing him past obstacles on the ramp, racing him past the bulldozer, and carrying him into the mountain's dark side. There they slowed down.

It was a wide passage, low-roofed and sloping upward steeply; and though it had been a blackness before, now it was faintly light. It must be true that the light came from the Nyols. The passage turned and twisted in much the same way that the caverns had done, and like the cavern, it seemed to twist through solid rock. Yet once or twice Simon thought there was a washing of soil across the rock floor, as though water had carried it there in a storm. He wondered if the passage was sometimes a river and imagined waterfalls spilling past the bulldozer, over the shelf where it stood, and far down into the dark heart of the mountain. He would have liked to look for signs of it, but the Nyols closed around and pressed him on.

They came around a turn and into a stretch that was

suddenly much lighter. It was dim gray light, but to Simon's dazzled eyes it seemed bright. He could see the stone-gray skins of the Nyols, and the uneven roof of rock pressing down. He shivered, feeling as if the monstrous old mountain held him crushed in a fist and thinking how deep inside it he had been.

Another turn—and the wind curled gently around him, and the daylight was so bright that he shut his eyes. The Nyols chuckled; they were quite good-humored again. With a last rush they carried him forward—and left him. Simon opened his eyes and shut them again. He was in a wide, shallow cave full of brilliant light. There was blue sky outside and, he thought, treetops.

It took a minute or so of opening and closing his eyes before he could see well again. Then, warned by the treetops, he went carefully to the edge of the cave and looked out. But the Nyols had not, after all, left him stranded as they had found him. The sloping ground of Charlie's bulge was just below, and the treetops rose from beyond it. To the right he could look far down on the ridge where the men were still clearing. The shadow of the mountain stretched over it; by mountain time it was late afternoon.

He had spent his lunch to buy two minutes in the bulldozer, and Simon suddenly knew he was very hungry. Also, it must be late enough for Charlie to begin to worry. He would have to hurry. Yet he couldn't help pausing to see how the Nyols might have brought the bulldozer to this narrow slope and along it and into the passage. He was sure that a person couldn't have done it; and now the bulldozer was inside the mountain for good. It could never come out—but he might go back some time with a torch to see it—if only the Nyols weren't so touchy. He turned away and hurried off around the mountain's rocky shoulder, coming face to face with Charlie.

Charlie's face was deeply creased, but as soon as he saw Simon, it relaxed into its usual lines. "There you are, then," he said. "Thought you might be having a bit of trouble. What happened? Did you find anything?"

Simon burst into speech. "I found them—the Nyols— a whole bunch of them! Strong! I bet even a gorilla couldn't wrestle with them. Where do you think I've been, Charlie? Right inside the mountain! Did you know it was all hollow in there, with miles of caves and stuff? Miles inside, of course. And you couldn't guess what's in there! Have a try—you wouldn't guess in a hundred years! The bulldozer's in there! They've got it!"

"You've had a day of it," observed Charlie with a serious inward smile. "Had your lunch yet?"

"No, I had to give it to them, and I'm starving."

"No lunch? It's past three. We'll go home for a cup, and you can tell us all about it."

Simon was only a little surprised that Charlie should be giving up his watch so soon. He was too excited to think much of the Nargun; and too glad to be out in the wide-open world again, where the silence was alive instead of hollow or dead. He poured out his story all the way down to the house and then, while Edie supplied bread and butter and cake to stop the ache inside him, he had to tell it all over again to her.

She was a satisfying audience. She didn't say much, but her face showed the wonder that Simon felt. She glanced once or twice at Charlie, who listened to the second telling as closely as the first.

"It just shows," she said at last. "We've never known any of that, even when we've known the other old things so long. I'll never be able to look at the mountain again without seeing the inside too. Stalactites, you said, Simey. And the bulldozer in there, and all those Nyols . . . Shouldn't be surprised, I suppose, after the Nargun. I suppose you didn't find anything new about *that,* Charlie?"

Then Simon did wonder about Charlie's deserted post. Some of his own excitement ebbed away, and the coldness of the Nargun came closer. He waited as Edie did for Charlie to answer.

"I might've," said Charlie.

"Go on, then," said Edie, while Simon was still looking astonished.

"Well, I don't know that there's time," said Charlie, "what with this long tale of Simey's. You did a good job, mate, and we'll go and have a look at that 'dozer one day; and you got a bit that ties in with mine, too. But it's getting late, and there's wood to chop and the rest. I want to go up there again with the tractor just on dusk, and I don't want to be caught up there in the dark. So I reckon we'd better get busy now and talk later."

"The tractor!" cried Simon. "You said we wouldn't touch it, Charlie!"

"Cool off, I'm not going to touch it. I just want to try something."

"You can go any time," said Edie. "I've chopped wood before. I'd rather break up a bit of wood and know what's going on. You ask a lot, Charlie."

He looked at her in a helpless way and sat back in his seat. "Sorry. I'm doing my best, that's all, and maybe I'm not too good at it. I'm trying not to put too much on you, Edie, and to have the young bloke by me and keep the lot of us safe. That's all. You look after the stock again, and I'll chop a bit of wood before I go."

"You'll do what's best. Tell me now."

"Well . . . I watched that thing like I said. I put Simey on his way and found a spot just above it, and I never took my eyes off it for four solid hours except to fetch my lunch. I'd have stopped longer only I got a bit anxious about the boy. And then he had that bit of a hint, and it seems to tie in . . ."

Edie nodded. "What did you see?"

"Nothing, maybe—only it happened every time. They were blasting a few trees. You'd have heard them."

Edie nodded again. "Never any warning. Heart failure every time."

"Five trees, they blasted. I got a shock myself the first time, didn't keep my eyes fixed tight enough. But I thought that stone thing shivered."

"Shivered?" wondered Simon. "You mean jumped the same as you did?"

"Well, it could've been that. I told you I jumped. Only

I thought it shivered. And I didn't jump the next time, and it did the same then. So then I thought it might be vibration through the ground, and I shifted a bit. Got it lined up with another rock and watched them both. That one never moved. Can't be sure, of course . . . But I *think* with every shot of jelly that other thing shivered."

11

SIMON WAS bewildered and almost ready to be angry. After the sheep and the fright with Surprise, and whatever it was that had happened the other night—after what all the old things had told them—Charlie had spent a whole day proving that the Nargun shivered when an ordinary stone didn't.

"But *Charlie!* It's the *Nargun,* and the other one's just a rock! Why *shouldn't* it shiver?"

"Why should it mate? We got a rope tight around it, and it didn't shiver then—it just went for us. It didn't shiver when you chucked a lump of wood at it. It just chucked it straight back. Why should it shiver at the blasting?"

"It was frightened," said Edie. "Poor thing."

"Well, I *think* it didn't like it. Matter of fact, I don't think it liked the chain-saw much either. Didn't shiver the same, but I *think* it crouched down harder when the chain-saw started. You had to watch so close a man couldn't be sure."

"So what?" asked Simon, really wanting to know.

"So then I got thinking. It's some sort of coincidence that we found out about this Nargun just when they started clearing the scrub. *Either* it landed on Wongadilla just when the clearing started—and that's funny if it doesn't like it; you'd think it'd go somewhere quiet—*or* it was here already, and it only started moving about when the clearing started. So maybe, if we could make *enough* row we could send it off somewhere."

"Oh, I see—and then the Nyols said that bit about making thunder and shaking mountains!"

"That's it, mate."

"So what are you going to do, Charlie?"

"I'm just going to give it a bit of a test: maybe prove something, maybe not. Night's when it moves, and I'm not playing about with it in the dark. But most night things really wake up at dusk. If this thing shivered in broad daylight, I reckon it might do more than that at dusk; enough for us to see and be sure. So I thought if I took the tractor up at dusk, with Simey to keep his eyes peeled while I'm driving, we might see if the tractor was enough to make it move at night."

"Suppose it does?" said Edie.

"Well—*I* don't know. We've found out a bit more, that's all. Time enough to start thinking about it then."

"And you won't go messing about with it? Or getting off the tractor? And you'll keep a close eye on Simey?"

"Scout's honor, old girl, only like Simey says we've got to do something. Now I'm going to chop a bit of wood and get the tractor out. Shake it up, Simey, or we'll be too late."

While Charlie chopped, Simon carried wood into the kitchen and managed to squeeze in time for feeding the hens as well. While they worked, the color began to drain out of the world, ebbing west after the sun; hills stood tall and flat against the green glow of the sky. Simon thought of the great stone inside its gully, watching with the empty darkness that might be its eye while daylight drained away like water from a tub. He shivered. To be caught in the dark, rousing the Nargun—

Charlie had checked the fuel and oil in the tractor, which was standing as usual outside the shed. Now he started it, rousing it into a noisy jabber, and shouted to Simon above the noise, pointing at the draw-bar at the back. Simon understood that he was to stand on that and climbed on while Edie watched. Some day, he hoped, he would enjoy standing on this bar watching the big wheels turn while Charlie drove. They would be going for wood or something, and he would remember the first time he rode the tractor out to rouse the Nargun.

The tractor made more noise than he had thought it would, and the draw-bar bounced as if it wanted to shake Simon off. Yet still he wondered if the noise would be enough—and was this the very fastest they could go? Was it fast enough to get away if the big stone came at them like that other time? He would have liked to ask, but he didn't want to shout questions at Charlie's slouched back above the noise of the tractor.

At any rate, they reached the little gully in time: just as dusk was closing in, but while it was still light enough to see. Charlie stopped the tractor and turned as far as he could in his seat.

"Are you all right there, mate? Think you can hang on? I'd sooner not put you down anywhere—you might see better, but I'd rather we stuck together."

"I can hang on all right," said Simon, "but I can't see much in front of you. Not for watching if it shivers."

"We don't want to see it shiver, we've seen that. If that's the best we can do, we're wasting our time. What we want is a decent sort of movement that you *can* see."

"Well, if I stand on the far side and look over your shoulder . . ."

"That's the ticket. Keep your eyes peeled, and whatever you do don't fall off. Look out for some sort of movement that looks as if it's trying to get away from the tractor—but yell if you see anything at all."

"Won't you be watching too?"

"Far as I can, but I've got to drive. And keep an eye on the sides of the gully so we don't go too far in and get trapped. Unless that thing's started moving about already, it's only about ten yards up, near that breakaway. I'm going in now. Ready?"

For a moment Simon tried to find a reason for not being ready, but there wasn't one. So he closed his fingers hard, on the back of Charlie's seat with one hand and on the mudguard with the other, and said, "Right!" He leaned forward to see ahead while Charlie started up again and, revving the motor as much as he could, drove into the gully.

The sides of the gully began to rise, and Simon looked at them quickly to assure himself that the tractor could still climb out. He found himself going rigid and had to remember to loosen his knees so that he could balance. Charlie's back looked rigid too, and the way he was crouching forward sent Simon's eyes searching over his shoulder. Before he was ready, he saw the great stone, crouched in its familiar way against fallen earth on the east bank.

He couldn't see the muzzle or the dark eye, only the hump of stone in the fading light. It seemed very close, yet Charlie was going even closer. The engine stuttered loudly and Simon held his breath. Had the Nargun pressed deeper into the soil just then?

They were only ten feet away when the tractor stopped with its engine running; Charlie would go no closer. He revved the engine in short bursts, so that the tractor roared angrily at the monster. Simon was stiff with dread that the thing would move—and then it did. It heaved a little, strongly, as a spiny anteater does, and sank itself inches deeper into the bank. Simon's locked fingers flew open to tap Charlie on the shoulder. Charlie nodded, fumbling with the gears. They backed off and swung wide and away, wheels riding up one bank and down again. Simon's back tingled from being turned to the Nargun, and he peered over his shoulder in case its shapeless bulk came rolling or lumbering after them.

They roared out of the gully, and the vista of it faded into dusk. They ran on down the slope, and in a minute Charlie stopped the tractor. He swung down and stood looking back, waiting to see if anything emerged from the dusk behind them. Nothing moved.

"That's it, then," said Charlie with satisfaction. "We made it move."

Simon breathed for a moment, looking back too. Everything about him felt loose and limp. At last he said, "Did that count? Burrowing down like that? Maybe we can only make it burrow into the dirt—we'd never know where it might come up."

"That was good enough for me. It'll be up to us to make it move the right way next time. You've got to remember that it's not dark yet and we only used the tractor."

"It makes more noise than I thought it would."

"Got a cracked muffler," said Charlie smugly. "I *thought* it might come in handy."

"You could take it right off!" Simon suggested. "Like the bulldozer's! That'd make it a lot more vicious, wouldn't it?"

"Or we might send you back in there to fetch the 'dozer."

"That's no good. Even if you were good enough to

drive it along that track, the Nyols would never let you."

"Well, hang on again. We'll go home and tell Edie. We've got something to think about now."

They went roaring on down, the sky darkening over them and the tractor spitting sparks from its cracked exhaust, Simon looking over his shoulder at the black bulk of the mountain. All its features were veiled in dark, so that it was only a shape against the black-pearl, star-pricked glow of the sky. The Nargun would not come after them now, levering at the ground with stumpy limbs; but where in that black bulk of mountain was the bulldozer? If he had x-ray vision and could see inside the mountain, where would he see that other yellow monster? Somewhere up there near the hump, where the outer cave was? No—that was mad—there was all the long passage. He tried to trace it in his mind, looking at the outside of the mountain, and to trace the way the Nyols had brought him from its back. He was still taking backward looks and frowning when Charlie ran the tractor into its usual spot under a tree and stopped it.

"Edie'll know we're safe home, anyhow. Better hurry, we could do with a wash before dinner. What are you frowning about? Can't hear anything, can you?"

"Eh?" said Simon. "Oh, no. You don't hear the Nargun much till it yells. Charlie, you know when we went up the mountain this morning? Going up the steep bit? I bet you don't know what we were riding over! I bet we rode right over the bulldozer!"

"Yeah?" said Charlie. "Just as well Surprise didn't know."

"But it's funny, isn't it? Going up and down over the top of it without knowing."

"You were all turned around, you can't help it in caves. It could be anywhere. You don't want to stand there staring—Edie's waiting to hear what happened."

It had grown so dark that the stars hung close and brilliant. They fumbled through the gate to the back door, and Charlie pulled it open on yellow light, warmth, and Edie's face turned to them from the stove. Simon had one foot in the door when the night reached out and held them frozen. Sudden and savage came the Nargun's cry, bellowing down from the mountain, full of all time and the darkness between the stars. It held them at the door while it rang between mountains and died away. Charlie pushed Simon inside and shut the door.

"We made it angry," whispered Simon. He felt like a stone.

Up in the high gully the Nargun had raised its crooked shape to stand as men do. It had lifted its snout and cried in anger to the stars. The mountain stilled and hushed around it. The treetops were still where the Turongs peered and did not stir. The bushes were still where a bandicoot crouched with its long nose quivering. From small hidden openings in rock, the Nyols gazed, stilled by the cry of the stone. "Old one . . ." they whispered. Only a rabbit, its terror too strong, made a shuddering

145

leap from the bank. The Nargun moved a limb with the pounding speed of its anger. The rabbit did not squeal before it was crushed.

In this hush the Nargun heard its own cry bellowing around the world and spinning into space. It felt earth shake on its path, its moth-wings falter, and saw the stars shaken like beads on their thread of silence. Since first it oozed from rose-red fire into darkness—since it saw light —in all of endless time—the Nargun had never been beaten at as it had tonight in the quiet time of waiting for the stars. Since first it felt the rhythm that was wrong and not the earth's, never had that rhythm been so close or so defiant. And the anger of the Nargun had shaken the universe.

It pounded at the ground with hard, angry limbs. It cried again, *Ng-a-a!*—and stars shook and earth faltered. It climbed its gully and broke through blackberries into the lonely place beyond; and there, in time, the calm voice of silence reached it, and the cold, forever light of the stars. It grew quiet and felt again the deep slow throb of earth, and it dreamed of fire. SIMON, said the lichen on its base; but the Nargun did not know.

The Turongs went leaping from bough to trunk, back to their scrub above the swamp, whispering among leaves. The Nyols rustled like bats inside the mountain and soon were chuckling. The bandicoot dug out a wood-grub. In time even Simon stirred by the fire, and the cane chair broke into tiny crowd-noises.

"*Twice,*" he said. "We made it angry . . ." Yellow

flames, darting up the chimney like little clutching hands, were reflected in his eyes.

"We've got to do more than make it angry," said Charlie. "We've got to make it go." The lines of his face had deepened with useless thinking.

Charlie and Edie had thought of charges of gelignite set along the top gully and fired in sequence, to chase the Nargun off. But this, like any other scheme, would have to be carried out at night in the Nargun's time for moving.

"Not safe," said Charlie. "You couldn't see where the thing was, to set off the right charge. And I don't like playing with jelly at night."

Edie added, "If you made a mistake and the thing got blown to bits, we'd have half a dozen Narguns instead of one."

"Anyhow," Charlie finished, "I couldn't lay a trail of jelly even one mile outside Wongadilla. No use sending it over the line and waiting for it to come back."

They had thought of using fire to coax the old thing away but had given up that idea more quickly. There was only a chance that the Nargun would respond; and even if it had been a certainty, they could hardly burn out miles of country beyond Wongadilla.

They had thought of chasing it away with the tractor. "If that was enough to make it move in half-light," said Edie, "you might do better at night. And you'd have the headlights to work by."

"There again," argued Charlie, "I can't go after it a hundred miles or so in the tractor. What it needs is some sort of vibration strong enough to shake it up properly, scare it off so it never wants to come back."

That was when Simon, who had been staring at the fire all this time and listening to the night instead of to Edie and Charlie, said, "We made it angry," and Charlie said, "We've got to do more than that."

"You could take the muffler off the tractor," said Simon, because he couldn't think of anything new and he had already thought of that before the Nargun cried. "Then it'd be a really big noise." Neither Charlie nor Edie answered, so he looked up from the fire to see if they were silently laughing at him. Edie was only knitting with quick, troubled fingers. Charlie was frowning at Simon as if he were a hole in the air. Simon stared back defiantly.

"*What* was it you said?" Charlie demanded, still frowning and staring.

Simon stammered a bit. "Th-the muffler. Off the t-tractor. To make more noise."

"Not that. Before, earlier. Something about the bulldozer."

Simon searched his mind. Muffler—tractor—bulldozer—"The muffler's broken off the bulldozer," he offered. "The exhaust was rusted through, and the passage is pretty low in some places, so I s'pose—"

"That's it. That's more like it. That'd make a powerful vibration."

"But you can't get the bulldozer *out*," said Simon.

"I don't want it out. You mightn't hear it much in there, but I reckon you'd feel it all right. 'Specially if you

148

were a Nargun. Did the 'dozer seem to be all right, apart
from the muffler? Could I start it?"

"No," said Simon promptly. "I mean there's nothing
wrong with it that I could see, unless it's out of petrol. But
you couldn't start it. I told you before. The Nyols wouldn't
let you. You don't know what they're like. They're all
over you, hundreds of them, like a giant octopus or something."

"M'p," said Charlie, and settled another log on the fire.
"What made you think the bulldozer was this side of the
mountain?"

"Because it is," said Simon simply. Under Charlie's eye
he began to justify this. "See, we went in from the *back*
of the mountain, and it was a long way, and it bent about
a lot, but mainly it went up and down. I mean it didn't
curl right around or anything. Mainly we kept going
toward the front of the mountain, see? And when we went
into the passage, I sort of knew we were going the other
way—back to the *back* of the mountain—I thought they
were going to leave me stuck where they found me. And
when we came out, it *was* facing the way I thought only
not as *far* as I thought. We came out on the *side* of the
mountain. So the passage must have started from pretty
close to the *front*. Like where we ride up."

Charlie stared at him for a long time, and he stared
obstinately back. This went on until Edie said, "Does it
matter where it is?"

Charlie came out of the staring, which must really have
been deep thinking, and said, "Not much. Better if it's

149

where the boy thinks, though. One thing, anyhow: either that passage is so steep that he couldn't have climbed out and he'd still be inside the mountain, or the bulldozer's not too deep down." He stared at the fire while Edie waited and Simon shifted and the cane chair shrieked in whispers, and at last he began to talk.

"It's just what we want, really. The bulldozer makes about ten times the noise of the tractor, and a lot more without its muffler. Shut inside the mountain and not too far down, it ought to be enough to shake the ground. Not like an earthquake, but so you'd feel it in your feet. Scare this Nargun into a fit, I reckon, a whole mountain shaking under it. Ought to be enough to make it clear out for good. It'd keep on shaking, you see, not just coming and going like the blasting."

"Make it come rushing straight down here," said Edie grimly. "Why should it climb up over a shaking mountain? It'd just rush down this way."

"Maybe," said Charlie, and stared at the fire again. After a minute he added, "Unless the tractor was cutting it off, driving about with *its* muffler off and its lights on. That ought to send this Nargun up the gully and down the back of the mountain."

Simon was enthralled. This would have been right, he knew. The bulldozer—another monster—dim and secret inside the mountain, unleashing its full roar. The whole mountain shaking: that was a plan big enough for the Nargun, if only it could have been done. He gave a deep sigh. "If only those Nyols would clear out! Just for a little while!"

"We'll sleep on it," said Charlie. "If it's still a good scheme in the morning, we'll go and see the Potkoorok again. Maybe it's no good with Narguns, but at least it ought to know something about Nyols."

12

THEY ALL SLEPT, because they were tired out, but Simon's sleep was haunted by the Nargun's anger. He thought of Charlie's plan as soon as he woke, and it still seemed good to him: an immense plan, big enough for a Nargun, if only the Nyols could be got rid of while Charlie started the bulldozer.

To Charlie, a bulldozer was not much more than a very big tractor; by morning the plan seemed uncertain, wild, and—worst of all—outlandish.

"A good thing, then," said Edie, at her calmest. "Fits the Nargun to a T. Have you thought of anything better?" And Charlie had to admit that he had not.

He felt more hopeful soon. At first light, after a quick cup of tea, he and Simon went to the top gully to check on the Nargun's position for the day. Charlie would do this every morning now, and Simon hurried into two sweaters and two pairs of socks so that he could go too.

Only the tops of the western hills were tipped with red-gold sunlight when they reached the gully. The grass was gray with late frost, crunchy to walk on and slippery under the horses' hooves. The air stung like cold water.

They rode up the gully till the sides were becoming too steep for horses to climb. Then they rode out of it, tethered the horses, and worked their way further up on foot, looking down over the banks. They passed the sharp bend and the screen of blackberry before they saw the Nargun. It was leaning back against walls of rock and staring at the sky. It was the first time they had looked at the dark emptiness of its crooked stone face, and they did not look long. They went quickly and quietly back to the horses.

"There you are, then," said Charlie, almost excited. "We've made it move—we've sent it back to hide."

Simon could say nothing. He was too shaken. That granite face turned to the sky seemed to bear all age, all emptiness, all evil and good; without hope or despair; with rocklike patience. He was shaken by a sudden storm of pity and fear.

"We'll have a bite of breakfast," said Charlie, "and go and find the old Pot-K. *After* we've got the jobs done. It's putting too much on Edie, all this business."

"She'd rather," Simon reminded him. "She likes to be in it as much as she can."

"M'p," said Charlie. "She'll be in it, all right. Who do you think will be driving the tractor while I'm starting the bulldozer?"

Simon was silent again, this time with astonishment.

He thought of Edie driving the tractor, bunched up in the seat with her bony feet reaching for clutch and brake. And the Nargun, they hoped, would be on the move nearby. "Someone'll have to be with her!" cried Simon.

"You," said Charlie. "And see you don't let her make friends with the brute and try to bring it home."

"She couldn't! Even the Turongs—even the *Nyols* aren't friends with it!"

"You never know with Edie," said Charlie. "With you either, maybe."

When jobs were done and breakfast over, they went to the swamp. The sun lay on it, and the floating weeds were a gay young green flushed with pink, ready for spring. Frogs creaked like a chorus of rusty hinges. Sitting on the bank while Charlie talked to the Potkoorok, Simon was swept away from them on a wave of longing: for a quiet day like this one, but without anything wrong; for a day when he could splash about in the swamp and perhaps be tripped up by the Potkoorok and perhaps coax it out with an apple.

He was thinking this against the background of Charlie's talk when something cool and heavy rasped softly over his hand as it lay on the bank. He looked, moved, and yelled, all in a moment: a black snake lay across his hand. As he yelled, it vanished, and the Potkoorok chuckled. Simon rounded on it angrily.

"You want to watch it! What if I died of fright?"

The Potkoorok chuckled again and turned its old lizard eyes on Charlie. "The Potkoorok tricks men and boys

154

and Nyols," it said smugly. "Most old things it cannot trick. Not Turongs, for they are tricksters too. Not Narguns, for they see with different eyes: less, and more deeply. Nyols are like boys. The Potkoorok could trick the Nyols, even out of their rocks. But this is a wrong thing. An old one does not trick another old one. We trick men."

"You want the Nargun to go, don't you?" Charlie argued.

"Why should I want that? The Nargun should go, yet this is not a trouble to the Potkoorok. My territory is here."

This self-satisfied point of view would have driven Simon to fury; but Charlie held on to his patience with the skill of experience. "What about the Turongs, then? Can they trick the Nyols?"

"Maybe. Not so good as the Potkoorok. They cannot help it."

"It ought to be the Turongs, Charlie," Simon broke in. "It means going right up to the end of the mountain, and the Turongs go up there all the time. They go everywhere. The Potkoorok couldn't go as far as that, could it?" He said this quite innocently because he had been wondering about it, but the Potkoorok bridled at once and looked indignant.

"How wise is the Boy!" it snapped. "Six times he sees the sun rise over Wongadilla, and already he knows what the Potkoorok knows! I have wasted ten thousand suns. I should have asked the Boy."

Charlie gave his mouse-colored hat a tug. His face was wooden. "Simey's got a point," he said comfortably.

A red light flashed in the Potkoorok's golden eyes. "Hear the Man in Charge! No wonder the Boy is wise, for the Man is his teacher. And did you take the Potkoorok's road into the dark places, Boy? Did you see with your eyes and hear with your ears? There were Turongs in the place of the Nyols?"

"Lay off, can't you?" Simon protested. "You just *said* this was your territory."

"And what is this, and what am I that live here? A Bunyip that lives in a swamp? And what is that, that runs in the far gully below? Another swamp, maybe?"

"It's a creek. And it doesn't go anywhere *near* the Nyols, if you want to be clever."

"Never let the Boy call the Potkoorok clever. Only the Turongs are clever, for they live in trees and are seen in rocks. Tonight the Boy will show this wonder to the simple Potkoorok, for you will travel with me to trick the Nyols."

"Hang on—" said Charlie.

"All *right*, I *will*," shouted Simon, exasperated.

Suddenly the Potkoorok began to chuckle. Its chuckles lapped and rollicked around the swamp, and the frogs doubled their cries at the sound. The Potkoorok lay on the bank and flapped its large green feet in the air, chuckling till its eyes streamed. "A trick—" it spluttered. "A trick—they will tell it across the land for a thousand years! In wells and streams and in secret waters under the

156

desert, they will tell how the Nyols fled from their rocks! I will be known forever, Boat Boy! They may even hear of you!"

"That's all very well," said Charlie, "but you'll have to manage without Simey. I'm not having him dragged along to prove how clever you are."

By now Simon was full of doubts and worries; but if Edie could drive the tractor across the path of the Nargun . . . He said, a little unwillingly, "Well, then, how will you know when the Nyols have gone, Charlie? They won't all go down the passage, see; they're not *solid* like the Nargun. They go through little places you can't even see, and a lot of them'll go out the back of the mountain probably. So how will you know when you can get to the bulldozer if I'm not there to come and tell you?"

"I don't even know if he can *swim!*" roared Charlie to the chuckling water-spirit. By now it was enchanted with its plan and full of good humor. It stopped chuckling and answered Charlie gently.

"When he travels with the Potkoorok, he can swim. In the water and the deep places he can breathe. When he looks with the Potkoorok, he can see and find the road. He will come to no harm, but keep him if you will. At sundown the Potkoorok goes to trick the Nyols out of their rocks. If the Boy is here then, he comes too." It slid away into the water, and the swamp chuckled.

"Look here, Simey," said Charlie, as they rode home, "we've got enough on our hands without the worry of this. We'll just let the old thing get on with its own job, and we'll get on with ours. Edie and I'll be needing a hand."

But Simon too had been enchanted—by the Pot-koorok's promise. "All right," he said gruffly. "Only how *will* you know when it's all right to go in to the bulldozer?"

Charlie rode in silence for a while. Then he said, "Wouldn't you be a bit upset going under the water with the old thing? It can be as silly as a wet hen—lord knows what it'll be up to."

"Not after it promised!" Simon cried. But Charlie did have enough on his hands without this extra worry, so Simon made himself speak sensibly again. "See, I'd be out to you with the message before you went in, so I'd still go down to Edie and do whatever else you want. Only I'd do this first. But it's up to you. I'll do what you say."

"Well . . ." said Charlie, sounding bothered. "We'll see what Edie thinks."

When Edie heard of the plan, she too seemed uncertain and asked if Simon could swim. He said that he could a bit, but it didn't matter, and explained about the Pot-koorok's promise. Edie was silent for a moment, retreating into a deep calm. At last she said, "I'd rather trust him with the Potkoorok than with those Nyols yesterday when we'd never even seen them. He'll be all right, I suppose." So Simon assumed that it was settled and he would go.

He had doubts himself as the day went on, growing less and less real by the hour. Soon everything seemed like the sort of dream where things go on happening whether you want them to or not, and you have no choice about what you will do. Listening to Charlie's instructions to Edie and himself about the tractor, helping to overhaul it and remove the muffler, taking a can of fuel and some oil up to the cave for the bulldozer—all of it seemed like some game of make-believe.

"What if the bulldozer won't start, Charlie?"

"It's a washout, and we'll have to think of something else. We won't know till we try."

"What if the Nargun stays right up where it was this morning? Will it hear the tractor?"

"It won't matter. The tractor only matters if the thing tries to come down. Now mind, you're not to go up the gully, just across and back below it. Just to keep that thing from coming down this way. Leave the rest to the bulldozer. I'll get back to you as quick as I can."

"Aren't you going to stop with the bulldozer, then?"

"Not if it's running all right. I'll leave it set on half-throttle and come back in case you and Edie strike any trouble. The fact is," said Charlie, "if you and Edie could cope with the 'dozer, I'd sooner have you in there than out here. Safer."

"You wait till you see the 'dozer," said Simon. "Perched right on the edge of that shelf. It could easy run over, and then it's some drop."

"M'p," said Charlie. "Put a couple of chocks of wood for the tracks with that can."

Meals were all wrong, too. Lunch was a hot dinner so that Edie needn't cook later in the day, and afternoon tea included fried eggs in case it was really late before they could eat again. After that Simon changed into swimming trunks and an old sweater, feeling as though a curtain were going up on some fantastic stage. Charlie and Edie were getting the evening jobs done when he called good-bye and started up the ridge. They both stopped what they were doing and watched him go.

"I'll take something warm up for you!" called Edie, and he waved. They had been through all that; it was only a way of saying good-bye. At least nobody had said, "Now mind you do just what the Potkoorok tells you." He turned off the track and ran, in his old spoiled tennis shoes, to the swamp.

The sun was dipping behind the tallest hills when he sat on the bank above the deep hole to wait. The water there looked dark and cold, and Simon shivered. He had to wait ten minutes before the water swirled and the Potkoorok's head appeared. It chuckled when it saw him and called, "Come, Boy!"

Breathing quickly, Simon went down the bank and into the pool. The cold water gripped his ankles and feet. He had to keep his eyes and his faith fixed on the Potkoorok in order to walk forward. When the cold had gripped his knees, the spirit said, "Look down now." Simon looked down into the pool. Through clear brown water he saw again the dim yellow shape of the grader.

"Take care," said the Potkoorok. "Follow after me." It sank gently down past the center of the frame, and Simon took one step forward and began to sink after it. They went slowly down, between the sideways-tipped cabin and blade, past the wheels, past the sign that said GRADER, down far underneath it to soft mud that swirled like smoke about their feet.

The shock of cold disappeared; the water was warmer than the air above. The hole was very deep. It could easily have drowned the grader too deep ever to be seen if the frame had not been so long that it spanned the deepest part. As it was, Simon looked up and saw the grader like a strange yellow scaffolding above him.

The water swirled in silk ribbons around his legs and face. He could feel it in his nostrils and ears just as you always can when your head is under water. The only difference was that he felt no need either to hold his breath or to breathe and that he could see a little, as if he were wearing dark goggles of wavy glass.

The Potkoorok was waiting for him at one side of the pool, patting at the wall with a webbed hand. He went to it across the heavily swirling mud and put his hand on the wall too and felt hardness under spongy moss. The hole went down into rocks. The Potkoorok spoke near his ear, and he heard it quite plainly.

"Down between rocks the water goes to feed the creek. We do not go that way."

Simon nodded, not wanting to talk in case that spoiled his feeling of not needing to breathe. He followed the Potkoorok along the rocky wall until it slipped into a cranny in the rock and disappeared. He went in after it and found that he had to crawl into a small tunnel of rock, full of water and sloping upward. He could just see a swirl in the tunnel where the Potkoorok waited.

It was like crawling into a large pipe full of water, except that the rock was rougher to crawl through. After a few yards the tunnel grew a little higher; Simon could lift his head above water and see the Potkoorok's head bobbing in front. In spite of its promise he could see no more than he had inside the mountain with the Nyols, but he saw its frog-face turn and grin at him.

"Now we breathe," it said, its voice hollow in the rock pipe. Wherever the air was coming from, it was true that Simon could breathe quite normally.

The tunnel grew higher and broader, the water shallower. Yellow-gray hairweed flowed delicately at its edge, and once he saw a pale spider flicker over the rocks. He saw the water licking at the edge of a crack and remembered at last the cold, clear note of drips in the Nyols' caverns. So of course the Potkoorok could travel into the mountain, and the Turongs could not. He was just thinking this when the Potkoorok spoke to him over its shoulder.

"This is the Potkoorok's road that runs many ways. How far will you travel with me, Frog Boy? Will you go where the rivers vanish into secret places of earth and rock? Would you swim in a dark, deep lake and rise through a pipe into the desert? Or should we go under all the wide land to the far west sea?"

"No, thanks," said Simon. "I'd rather see you trick the Nyols." He felt again as though a mountain held him in its

162

fist, and something with a lot of legs had just run over his hand.

The Potkoorok chuckled happily. "That will be a trick! You will not break it with a word or a cry or a question. You will watch and follow and be silent; and when the time comes, you will run quickly to tell the Man."

"All right, I know that," said Simon.

"Follow me now," said the creature, and slithered into a crack so narrow that Simon almost lost faith in it and turned back.

It was the worst thing he had ever had to do, to force himself into that narrow crack in the dark, deep rock. He did it quickly because he had to—because he must not lose the Potkoorok for so much as a minute—because alone he could not see or breathe or move about here; and once he tried, a slime of weed helped him to slide through. The crack opened wider so that he could move his arms about and see ahead. The Potkoorok was waiting, sitting in the center of a leaf-shaped tunnel.

A trickle of water ran down the center of this tunnel, over a bed of black slime. The Potkoorok, sitting on the slime, called, "Now the road is fast!" It pushed with its hands on the rock and went sliding away down the tunnel. Simon tried, too, and found himself sliding after it. He shouted a question.

"If the water keeps running away like this through the rocks and creeks, why doesn't the swamp run dry?"

The Potkoorok fell out of the tunnel with a splash into

a pool in a small cave. It waited for Simon to splash down beside it. Then it said severely, "Is the Boy blind? Why does the swamp lie high on the mountain? What makes the swamp?"

Simon wished that it wouldn't talk in questions whenever it felt important or superior. He answered with some irritation. "Well, the mountain catches a lot of water, and I suppose it runs off and lies there. It's so high—I suppose even the dew . . ."

"That is a place for a Bunyip, not for a Potkoorok. A place for rotting and mud, not for clean water flowing—"

"Springs!" cried Simon. "There are springs running into it!"

The Potkoorok rose solemnly from the pool. "The birthplace of many streams," it said. "Not a swamp, but a dreaming of rivers." It led the way out of the cave into a corridor.

Simon followed, turning over another thing that he somehow knew was right. He remembered the day he first saw the swamp, lying so high on the mountain, and how he could hardly believe it was true. He had known it could not be an ordinary swamp; of course, it was the birthplace of rivers.

Close at hand he heard the cold bell-note of water falling drop by drop into a pool. The Potkoorok waited for him to come close and bubbled quietly into his ear.

"Soft as a ripple, Boy. No talk. The Nyols have good ears."

13

THE POTKOOROK went striding lightly ahead, and Simon crept after it. He was so close that he thought he could feel the creature shaking and began to feel afraid himself —until the Potkoorok stopped to lean against the rock, and he saw that it was chuckling. It leaned back, pressing its flat fingers over its large mouth for silence, and shook with inward chuckles. Simon waited crossly, unable to share the joke. When it could control itself, it leaned close to Simon and bubbled into his ear.

"Now you will see a trick! No words to break the thought. Watch and follow."

"Get on with it, then," Simon hissed back. He was sure they had been a long time already, and Charlie and Edie were waiting out there with the Nargun. It was no time for the Potkoorok to stand about gloating.

It went forward with bobbing strides into a cave where water lay. Cold drips fell on Simon as he followed it into a shallow pool where it squatted like a frog, closed its eyes, and seemed to dream.

Simon squatted beside it, waiting anxiously for it to move again. They were still a long way from the Nyols, he thought. The rocks about the pool were damp, and water dripped from overhanging ledges, sounding its bell-notes in the pool. How many drips, he wondered, made a pool? And did they fall faster in wet weather, ringing a chime in the dark? While he was looking, the rock walls seemed to waver; all about the cave, water was sliding stealthily down them from ledges and cracks. The pool was deepening—he could feel the water creeping coldly up and up his chest. He looked anxiously at the water-spirit; it still squatted with its eyes closed and a frog-smile on its face. He opened his mouth to call out and shut it again. He was not supposed to speak, so he wouldn't—yet.

Quickly the water deepened, and slowly, dreamily, the Potkoorok stretched out and began a crawling swim. Simon half swam and half crawled after it. They went with the water out of this cave and into another; and as they went, the water swirled and rose. For a moment Simon knew that this was the Potkoorok's trick. There could not be enough water to flood the caves so quickly. It was not real; yet it was more real than a picture; it was happening to him in his mind.

He was crawling or walking, yet it felt like swimming. The rocks were dry, yet he could see their wetness and feel the silken swirl of water. Ahead, the Potkoorok must be bobbing as it walked, yet he could see its head bobbing on the water. He stopped wondering at this dream that was happening to him and gave himself up to it. . . . He was swimming through the heart of the mountain in dark and winding caves; and the water swirled higher and stronger, carrying him on.

Now there was a whisper of water against rock and a clucking and chuckling around pillars. In dark reaches there were lappings and splashings that echoed and ran about. The Potkoorok chuckled, and all the winding caverns were full of the sounds of water. Suddenly there was another sound, like the rumble and slide of stones: the chattering and soft cries of Nyols.

The Potkoorok swung close to the rocks, and the strong flow of water drew Simon after it. They were carried on close under ledges and behind fretted pillars of crystal. The rumble of voices lined their way from above, but they turned their faces down and never looked up to see. The voices were startled, excited—disturbed like bees if you knock on their hive with a stick—but not frightened. The undreaming part of Simon's mind began to doubt that the trick would work.

The rock beneath them sloped up sharply; Simon had to lie at full length to pull himself along under water. They were coming to an end of the flood. It swirled past them on this rising rock to lie deep and dark in a broad cavern. On the far side it moved about a broken reef of rocks with a quiet lapping that was clear in the imprisoned silence. On the reef swarmed a crowd of Nyols, rum-

167

bling and muttering and clambering over each other to look. Above them stretched a pier of rock where more Nyols crouched to look down; and behind them, rich in the dimness, was the yellow shape of the bulldozer. Simon and the Potkoorok were aground on the ramp of rock that led up to it; they had come on the flood right through the mountain to the Nyols' meeting place.

The Potkoorok squatted in shallow water with its eyes closed and the dreaming smile on its face. Sometimes it chuckled, and the lapping and clucking of water went through the cavern and off through the heart of the mountain. Simon crouched beside it watching: the dark spread of water where the Nyols crouched, and the darker reaches flooding away, and the yellow bulldozer looming above. Nyols dangled each other from rocks to touch and feel the water, making splashing noises. They went scuttling and swinging like monkeys along rock walls by little crags and ledges, coming and going through the mountain. Still they seemed angry and excited but not afraid; and still the Potkoorok sat dreaming.

After a time, from far away down corridors, came a flurry of movement and the suck and wash of water. Nyols went scurrying off along rocks, and the crowd thinned. Simon felt the shallow water rise a little, washing into the cave on some new tide. The cries of Nyols echoed out of the mountain, and now they did seem afraid. The water swirled and the cries came closer, passed from Nyol to Nyol. Simon began to hear what they said.

"A Great One comes!"

"Give room, give room!"

"The Rainbow Snake! It comes, it comes!"

"Go while the Rainbow Snake passes!"

The hair on Simon's neck and arms began to stir. He looked at the Potkoorok, smiling with closed eyes, and stayed still. The water pushed in with a great strong swirl, and sliding with it out of the darkness came something huge. A long gleaming body went looping through the cave. A great flat head, as thick as the trunk of a tree, lifted from the water and lowered again. With a rustling in rocks, the Nyols were gone; there were no more cries. Simon leaped up and went running up the ramp, past the bulldozer and away down the passage beyond.

What sight the Potkoorok had lent him stayed with him and stopped him from crashing into rocks; but as he ran, the dream trickery began to fade. Soon he was running with relief instead of fear, and at last he was running and stumbling to reach Charlie as quickly as he could. It seemed a long time before the beam of Charlie's flashlight painted a rock wall yellow; then he was in the outer cave, and the world was open before him with the light of evening on it, and stars beginning to prick through the glow of the sky.

"There you are, then," said Charlie tensely. "All right?"

"They've gone. You'd better hurry before they come back."

"Crazy scheme," said Charlie, tucking wooden chocks under the arm that held fuel and oil cans so as to leave a hand free to manage the flashlight. "I must've been mad. Edie's just below the little gully waiting for you; you'll see the tractor. There's another flashlight in my back pocket; better take it in case you want it. She says to hurry before you catch cold."

"Can you manage all that stuff? I could come in with you and help carry it. It's just right at the end of the passage, you'll see the bulldozer as soon as you get there, but watch the edge so you don't fall off."

"I'll be right," said Charlie. "You watch out for yourself and Edie, and I'll be with you as quick as I can. Off you go, now, and stick close to the fence as long as you can in case that thing's roaming about."

Simon found a small flashlight in the pocket that Charlie presented to him and picked his way down to the stony ground while Charlie watched. He waved his flashlight, and Charlie's waved back from the cave, and then Simon switched his off. It wasn't properly dark yet, and he didn't need a flashlight.

He hurried around the curve of the mountain till he reached the fence, climbed through it, and started down the steep fall holding on to the wire for support. He could hear the tractor idling, making a series of explosions, *phut . . . phut . . . phut,* because of not having a muffler. In the still evening it seemed almost loud enough to challenge the Nargun by itself. He flashed the light toward it once or twice so that Edie would know he was coming. A breeze as cold as the stars curled round his damp clothes.

Damp. Not wet. His sweater and trunks had dried out quite a lot on the way through the rocks. When he had thought he was swimming but was really walking or crawling. He knew now that the flood and the Rainbow Snake were not true, but it was hard to believe that they had not been true then. The Potkoorok had made them true. When all this was over he would remember it properly—make it part of his memory of the dark heart of the mountain; for it, too, was something that had happened to him there. Just now it was better to stick to things that were waking-real and to follow Charlie's plan step by step.

He had reached the easier slope of the mountain's lap. He could see the tractor's black shape lit now and then by the spitting of blue-orange flame from its exhaust. He hoped Edie would have the sense not to turn the headlights on and blind him, and of course she did have the sense. She met him a few yards from the tractor, coming out of the dusk with a bundle of clothes.

"There you are, then. All right? Get these dry things on—leave your wet ones somewhere till tomorrow." She patted him quickly here and there. "Nearly dry. I hope you haven't caught a chill."

Simon took the bundle behind a bush. The dry clothes felt warm and comforting on his damp skin. He shoved the flashlight into the pocket of the jeans, left his damp things where they were, and went back to the tractor. Edie was now sitting in her place looking as improbable as he had imagined. He climbed onto the draw-bar and leaned forward to speak into her ear.

"We're not to go into the gully, Charlie said."

She yelled the answer over her shoulder. "We're just going backward and forward across the mouth. And you're keeping your eyes skinned in case you see anything move. Hang on!"

She switched on the headlights. The tractor gave a series of ear-splitting explosions, *bang . . . bang . . . bang,* and then *bang-bang-bang* as it moved slowly forward west across the lap of the mountain. Edie was a jerky and hesitant driver; the draw-bar bounced and jerked, and Simon clung on for his life. A little way beyond the gully, she began to turn, showing a tendency to panic as the wheels turned downhill and picked up speed; the engine noise dropped to a *phut . . . phut . . . phut* while she forced the tractor around and rose to an anxious BANG-BANG-BANG as she hurried it back on course. They were running east toward the fence, passing the mouth of the gully, and going a little beyond.

Simon wondered how in this noise they would ever know that the bulldozer had started, if it did start. He supposed it would not matter if they never did know. What mattered was to search the gully and the dark face of the mountain for a black, misshapen mass that was coming the wrong way.

Edie went into her second turn, with the same moment of panic on the downhill run when the motor almost died and the same crescendo of bangs as they scrambled back on course. In the quieter moment Simon strained his singing ears for a sound of the bulldozer and heard none. The swinging headlights fanned out in front, and they were running west again.

Simon's eyes were screwed up with peering into the dark behind the lights. Passing the gully mouth, Edie peered too, slowing the tractor almost to stalling and then, to make up for it, bounding on past. In the stalling stage Simon listened as well as peered. He did not expect to hear anything, yet he listened with stretched ears.

He listened again at the turn, waiting for Edie's regular moment of panic while his eyes followed the sweep of the turning lights. Nothing that he could see; nothing that his singing ears could hear. Yet behind the noise of the tractor he felt again that stillness of the night when he had met the Nargun: that second when his mind and skin and blood all listened to the waiting silence.

They swung back east—and that was surely a flash of light from the end of the mountain? Charlie's flashlight? Simon banged Edie's shoulder and pointed. She nodded hard—she had seen it too. But now they were passing the gully, which they should have been watching instead of Charlie's light. Simon screwed up his eyes again; Edie slowed to a crawl while she craned anxiously; the tractor stalled. Silence closed on them like a trap.

"Curse!" muttered Edie, fumbling with the controls; and Simon whispered, "Shush! Not yet!" He stilled the singing of his ears to listen. There was something deep and strong, too low to hear: a *whmp, whmp, whmp* that was not his heart. Was that what he had felt in the silence?

Could it be the Nargun? He knew at once that it was not. Nothing about the Nargun had that machinelike regularity; it might be the bulldozer, perhaps. But what was that other sound that he could not hear? What else was there?

All his life and being reached out listening to the night. No feather floating down from any tree; no cricket moving under any stone. Was it the mountain stirring? . . . darkness flowing? What moved?

In one more heartbeat he knew. Edie had managed to to start the motor, *bang . . . bang . . . bang.* Simon shrieked, *"Edie! Jump!"* And the cry of the Nargun sprang at them from the gully.

Nga-a-a!

Simon leaped from the tractor and dragged at Edie, who was tumbling out. They dragged and pushed each other behind a tree while the great dark shape thudded at the tractor. Stumpy limbs crashed at metal, the motor spat and roared and died; headlights swung as the tractor toppled over. Rock fists smashed at it, and the Nargun raised its snout and bellowed at the stars.

Terror turned Simon's hands to steel, grasping at Edie and dragging her through the dark to a farther tree. They saw Charlie's flashlight wobbling fast across the mountain and that was another terror—he would go stumbling straight into the monster! Simon dragged out his own light and flashed it once; that was all he could do in case it brought the ancient monster thundering after himself and Edie. He crushed her against the tree, and her own hands were steel holding him there too. They breathed jerkily.

Charlie's light had vanished. There was darkness except for the overturned headlights; and then a tearing and leaping of flame that lit the gully mouth and made the trees jump. The tractor was burning, and the Nargun lurched erect in the flames and bellowed with pride. The stars wavered. Simon's heart leaped and shuddered as Edie did. He watched and listened as though every nerve was separately alive.

The flames grew ragged, leaping and falling so that the Nargun appeared and disappeared, at one moment rearing its crooked head to the stars, at another crouched low against the ground. Then, as the flames leaped again, it was moving: dragging itself with heavy power east along the mountain.

Simon and Edie inched each other around the tree. The fire was only a red glow making the darkness darker. Away from it, toward the fence, a dark uneven shape rose against the stars and dropped down again. Simon dared to flash his light once again for Charlie. His legs and arms were no longer steel but ordinary shaking limbs; and through his feet he could feel the *whmp, whmp, whmp* of the bulldozer. Edie was breathing fast.

They waited and heard nothing except a twanging of wires from the fence. Then there were trees swaying and hissing overhead: the Turongs were stirring excitedly. Soon after that Charlie's light flashed close by. Simon flashed back, and Charlie came stumbling out of the dark and grabbed at them both and felt them all over while they clung to him.

"You're all right, then. Worst ten minutes I ever spent. Never been so glad to see a flashlight. Had to wait till the thing went past before I could get here."

"Charlie, did you see? The tractor—"

"Blast the tractor. The thing's gone around the mountain. That fence would've done no good, it was making short work of the boundary when I left. I'm going after it to see what happens, but I'll see you both to the house first if you can make it. Or would you rather lie low somewhere here till you get your legs back?"

"We're staying together," said Edie. "We'll come."

"Well . . . are you up to it? We'll have to hurry."

"Better get a move on, then."

They went as quickly and quietly as they could, stopping now and then to look and listen. They saw no great misshapen shadow, but the *whmp, whmp, whmp* of the bulldozer grew stronger under their feet as they went. When they had passed between two leaning fence posts where broken wire lay slack and curled, they began to hear with their ears a booming that matched what they had felt in their feet.

"It's not too loud, is it?" whispered Simon. "What's it like inside?"

"Enough to bring the mountain down," said Charlie. "The passage is acting as a muffler. It's good enough to draw your Nargun, mate. That's where he's headed."

They crept on with greater care, sure that the Nargun would reach the outer cave but not sure how or when. Outside the cave Charlie took the risk of using his flashlight; its beam went prodding through the dark and found nothing. They could hear the bulldozer clearly. Charlie made Simon and Edie wait while he went into the cave. They waited tensely till he came to the edge and lit their way in with the flashlight.

The cave was empty. They moved nervously aside from the black hole that led into the mountain, pressing themselves against the rock and listening to the bulldozer's muffled boom.

"Put your ear on the rock," whispered Simon.

With their ears pressed to the rock, they could hear the big machine pounding and vibrating; Simon felt at last the power of that engine unleashed in full roar. A monster against a monster; it was worth that journey along the Potkoorok's dark roads. The bulldozer shouted a challenge—and underneath the shouting was another sound, just heard. The heavy grating of rock across rock as the Nargun went, slow and heavy, to meet the challenge.

"It's in there," whispered Simon. "What'll happen?"

"Not what we planned, anyhow," said Charlie. "And I'm not going in to find out. Bad enough with a flashlight and no Nargun."

They waited and listened, now one and now another putting an ear to the rock. Outside the cave the hills drew away, dark and tall against the sky, like giants thinking. Overhead were the far, cold stars.

Then, for the last time, they heard the Nargun cry.

Its cry came hollow from the passage, wild and savage as always; full of hate that was love, of love that was hate, centuries of emptiness, anger hungry to destroy. As always, Simon felt something curl up inside him. He had always thought it was naked fear, but now he was not sure. It might be naked pity. He pressed his ear to the rock as Edie and Charlie had done.

Into the thunder of the bulldozer came a dreadful jangling of rock against metal. The night air was sucked past them into the passage and came rushing out again. There was a great blast of sound, and in a moment a great blast of heat. Then came a thunder in the mountain's side, a shaking and rumbling that died little by little. After that there was silence, thick and dead.

They stood away from the rock, shaken and shocked. Charlie turned his flashlight into the mouth of the passage. A drift of dust curled and twisted, eddying into the cave.

"Rock's fallen in the passage," said Charlie to the stares of Edie and Simon. "Thought it might, with the vibrations. There was loose soil on the floor, and cracks above —I was glad to get out. I'll have a look tomorrow, but I reckon your Nargun's walled in for good."

14

TOWARD MORNING the Nyols came back, slipping into the mountain by their own invisible ways. First one or two came, shyly like shadows, afraid that their mountain might still be invaded and ready to flee in a moment—for the Rainbow Snake was one of those who had been worshiped by men, and small elf-spirits must make room for these great ones. When the first few who slipped between the rocks did not come out a few more followed, and others after those. Long before the eastern sky had begun to glow like a black pearl, hundreds of Nyols had crept inside the mountain.

In trees above, the Turongs dived and howled to each other. They had seen the defeat of the tractor and heard the battle in the mountain, and they quivered with curiosity. They scuttled like spiders in branches and peered slyly from leaves and learned nothing. By threes and fours and dozens the Nyols crept into the mountain and were silent.

They were silent with awe, for they found a mystery. Clustered like bats on ledges and galleries, they looked down and wondered. The great serpent had gone; the flood had gone, and all the caverns were dry and dusty as before. Crystal columns and frozen cascades sparkled through the dust. Pools were in their basins undisturbed, and dripping water rang its silver gongs. Only in the great cavern was there a change—and there—

There had been a great fire. Some mighty blaze had leaped from side to side, from high to low. The floor and roof were scorched and blackened; lizards and pale creeping things were dead in great numbers, and a strange and heavy smell hung in the cavern. Perhaps the Rainbow Snake had called the sun itself into the mountain? The rocks were still warm from fire; and to keep the mystery from men, the passage had been closed with massive rocks.

But there was something else that made the Nyols stare and whisper. Their great machine, as yellow as the sun, had fallen from its high place, smashed and blackened in the fire. Why was this? The Nyols stared and whispered from above and dared not come down.

And while they crowded on high ledges talking in soft rumbles, there came a sound: the slow, heavy grating of rock upon rock. The Nyols fell silent and stayed as still as stones. The sound in the mountain went on. They heard it pass from corridor to cavern, and by and by they crept and sprang like shadows in search of it.

They found the Nargun crawling down a corridor, turning its weathered snout from side to side in a blind search for light. It raised its crooked shape on stumpy limbs to look up at them, clustered on the walls above with their eyes shining darkly like very distant stars. They stirred and muttered, for now they thought they had found out the mystery.

This ancient stone creature, their dreaming, had come to them in the dark of the mountain. The Rainbow Snake had ruled that they should not keep their yellow machine; it was destroyed so that they might have the Nargun. They did not dare, yet, to come down from their high places; but when the monster lurched slowly on its way, they rustled after it along the walls like bats, and sometimes they crooned to it softly without words. They did not understand that it was searching, searching through all the caverns and corridors for a way out to the wind and to brighter, colder stars.

"Will it get out again?" Simon asked the Potkoorok. It had been into the mountain by its secret road to peep.

"There is no road for the Nargun," it said.

"Will it *ever?*"

"How long is ever? When the mountain crumbles; when a cave opens; when a man or a river breaks down the rock; is that ever?"

Simon shivered, thinking about it. "It *is* ever," he said at last. "But not now."

"Not now."

"*Poor* thing . . ." He sat up suddenly, and a dragon-fly hovering by his head like a tiny helicopter darted backward and away. "What about the bit that broke off and ran away? How long will it take to grow up?"

The Potkoorok, having finished its own apple, snatched Simon's and beamed with pride. Simon didn't notice. "How long?" he demanded.

"How long will the Boy be stupid?" the creature said pettishly; for a trick can hardly be called successful if the victim doesn't notice it. "Does stone grow? When the wind rubs over it and the rain beats at it and the frost squeezes it, does a stone grow bigger? The small Nargun will grow smaller. Watch your toes, Frog Boy, or one day they may be bitten." It crunched Simon's apple and rolled its golden eyes at him sideways. "When the big Nargun lay on the mountain, it too was squeezed by the frost. Rain and snow and sun it loved, and it opened its arms to the wind; it grew smaller day by day. The caves are still; no wind moves there, and nothing falls but dust. You have preserved your enemy."

"Only now it can't get out," retorted Simon. "Anyhow, a lot you care as long as you can boast about your marvelous trick."

At this the Potkoorok flapped its webbed hands with glee and chuckled till it fell backward on the bank kicking its feet. Since it had been doing this at intervals all the afternoon, and the sun was now behind the ridge, and since the apples were finished, Simon walked off and left it there.

All day the ancient Nargun had crawled and lurched through the mountain, searching for a way out. All day the Nyols followed it in wonder; and when it rested in a pool so that it might feel the water, they ventured lower down the walls and crooned to it shyly.

"Old one . . . " "Brother Stone . . ." "You stay . . ."

They could not have helped it if they would, for now the rocks in the passage were jammed under the weight of the mountain, and there was no way out for the Nargun. Nyols might come and go by their own roads; but earth, that was its substance, had taken back the Nargun.

It came out of the pool and lurched on its slow way, and the Nyols tracked it from above. It came again to the fire-blackened cavern where it had battled and silenced the great machine. Foot by foot it dragged itself to the twisted ruin, and there it leaned. Little by little the Nyols drew near, crooning happily.

"Brother . . ." "Old one . . ."

They brought broken crystal, fretted like the columns it had known before, and laid the pieces near it.

"We find you, we serve you . . ."

Small hands gathered dust and poured it gently over the monster, anointing it.

"You stay . . ."

They brought it small dead lizards, and their eyes flickered in the cavern like the first stars.

The Nargun never moved. In this place of nothing—
no light, no wind, no heat, no cold, no sound—it waited.
It felt the old, slow pulse, deep and enduring, and remembered the earth swinging on its moth-flight around the
sun. Its dark, vacant eyes waited: for the mountain to
crumble; for a river to break through; for time to wear
away.

SIMON, it said. But the lichen had withered, and the
name was only a whisper in the dark.